SERENITY AT 70, GAIETY AT 80

Why you should keep on getting older

GARRISON KEILLOR

also by Garrison Keillor

Boom Town, 2022

That Time of Year: A Minnesota Life, 2020

The Lake Wobegon Virus, 2020

Living with Limericks, 2019

The Keillor Reader, 2014

O, What a Luxury, 2013

Guy Noir and the Straight Skinny, 2012

A Christmas Blizzard, 2009

Pilgrims, 2009

Life Among the Lutherans, 2009

77 Love Sonnets, 2009

Liberty, 2008

Pontoon, 2007

Daddy's Girl, 2005

Homegrown Democrat, 2004

Love Me, 2003

In Search of Lake Wobegon, 2001

Lake Wobegon Summer 1956, 2001

ME, 1999

Wobegon Boy, 1997

The Old Man Who Loved Cheese, 1996

The Sandy Bottom Orchestra, 1996

Cat You Better Come Home, 1995

The Book of Guys, 1993

WLT, 1991

We Are Still Married, 1989

Leaving Home, 1988

Lake Wobegon Days, 1985

Happy to Be Here, 1981

SERENITY AT 70, GAIETY AT 80

Why you should keep on getting older

GARRISON KEILLOR

PRAIRIE HOME PRODUCTIONS · MINNEAPOLIS, MN

ISBN: 9781733074575
Library of Congress Control Number: 2021921752

Visit our website at garrisonkeillor.com

First Edition

Designed by David Provolo
Art direction by Helen Edinger

The year passes and the old man with the scythe
Is mowing closer. He hasn't been subtle, has he.
Every day a few more people say goodbye,
Which makes me want to be light-hearted, jazzy,
Put out the hors d'oeuvres and the champagne,
Sing *God Bless America, You Are My Sunshine,*
In My Life, Amazing Grace, Purple Rain,
I'll Be Your Baby Tonight, and *Auld Lang Syne.*
We've mourned for our dead and been sorry a
Long enough time. Now I take your hand, your
Eyes alight, and let us sing an aria
To love and beauty and youth and grandeur.
May the new year bring us before it has flown
What we would have wished for had we only known.

—G.K.

PREFACE

My life is so good at 79 I wonder why I waited this long to get here, so much of what I know would've been useful in my forties. Yes, there's loneliness and pain, despair, guilt, a sense of meaninglessness, the feeling of *Why am I here? What did I come in the kitchen for? A fork? A glass of water? A Pearson's Salted Nut Roll?*—welcome to the club—but on the other hand I'm not on a tight schedule or under close supervision so I have freedom to look around and think for myself. I look at the front page of the paper and think, "Not My Problem." The world belongs to the young, I am only a tourist, and I love being a foreigner in America. I wake up early and plant my bare feet on the floor and slip away quietly so as not to awaken the gentle sleeper next to me. I turn the coffeemaker on and do a few neck flexes and get in the shower and recite the Doxology or the 87 counties of Minnesota in alphabetical order (Aitkin, Anoka, Becker, Beltrami, Benton, Big Stone, Blue Earth, Brown, Carlton, Carver, Cass, Chippewa, Chisago, Clay, Clearwater, Cook, Cottonwood, Crow Wing, etc.) to rev up the brain and put on a black T, jeans, red sneakers, walk to the kitchen, pretending I'm on a tightrope, and take the medications that promise to thin the blood and stifle brain seizures and I drink a cup of coffee and sit down at the table and feel grateful for the day to come. Life is good as your future diminishes; the scarcity makes your days more delicious. Instead of nostalgia, I feel the love of right now, this minute, 6:15 a.m. on my cellphone, so it's precisely that, except in saying so I've made it 6:16.

Either I'm in Minneapolis, looking out at St. Mark's and Loring Park where I walked at 18, on break from my job in a scullery, practicing smoking Pall Malls, intending to go to the U and become a writer, or I'm in Manhattan, looking at rooftops of brownstones on the West Side, three blocks from the restaurant where I met my wife in 1992, the younger sister of my younger sister's classmate Elsa, a three-hour lunch. Some mornings are bleary but nothing like back in my drinking days, 20 years ago. At 79, there is no time for a big grievous slump like when I was striving to be brilliant. Life is passing. Get to work. You've been doing this all your life, you know the drill. Shut the computer, get out paper and pen. You write and as you do, you cut, you scratch and replace, the garden grows by pruning. You hear the solid phrase as you write, and if you make four pages of scratches and scribble and get eight solid lines, it's a good start. Three hours later, Jenny appears. She sits on my lap, silently, my hand on her back. We are perfectly still for a minute. She pours a cup of coffee, lightens it with milk, looks at me. She says, "Good morning. How are you?" and I say, "Never better" and it's the honest truth, now that she's here.

I was a big shot once and journalists wanted to interview me, which was fun but nobody is that interesting for long and it's a comfort to become a tourist in old age, a sort of weightlessness, and enjoy my irrelevance. People resist vaccination mandates as the rate of infection increases: Not My Problem. Freighters wait to unload at ports, docks are piled with containers, supplies are running low, building projects are delayed: NMP. The local opera company, while doing *Don Giovanni* and *Carmen* this season pledges to challenge patterns of discrimination and privilege and exercise its moral imperative in behalf of inclusivity and diversity and bring about a sense of authentic belonging in opposition to systems of oppression and colonialism and suspicion of otherness, to which I say, "Goody goody gumdrops" though it is NMP. *I'm no longer from here.*

We reach old age through sheer good luck. We have the benefit of drugs unavailable to our grandparents and things surgeons do to your heart or hip or knee, we avoided drowning, close calls on the highway turned out in our favor, we didn't fall in with people whose hobby was opiates, we had mothers who told us to look both ways and we did. My cousin Roger drowned at 17 and dear friend Corinne at 43 and I think of them often, the tall kid with the flattop and the crooked grin, the serious economist who could be jollied into sitting at the piano and walloping out "On The Road To Mandalay," and I pick up my feet and march forward. The first step to a good old age is gratitude.

The Fall of Man, 1616, Hendrick Goltzius

As little kids, we all did hilarious imitations of elderly dither, the shaky hand, the quavery creaky voice ("Where is my Geritol?"), the stooped back and hesitant step, the forgetfulness and spooky dementia, and now here we are, the butt of our own joke. Perfect justice. What happened? We lost a stride, our vision blurred slightly, we hesitated at the stairway, someone asked, "Are you okay?" We said, "What? Sorry?" and an invisible sign *ELDERLY* was hung around our neck and people start going out of their way to be kind to us who never had bothered to before. I used to hold the door for women and now they hold the door for me and point out a treacherous curb and incline. I resent this. They are nice Christian women doing as Our Lord commanded, assisting the pitiful, but I'm not pitiful (yet) so please take your helping hand and help someone else. People say, "You're certainly looking natty," and I have to google the word, I never heard it before, it means, "decrepit but nonetheless presentable."

Matters go downhill fast. A stranger looks at you and speaks RATHER LOUDLY AND OVER-ENUNCIATES and you want to poke him in the snoot. You board the bus and a woman gets up and offers her seat. You don't want her goddamn seat, you're quite capable of standing on your own two feet, but to your surprise, you say "Thank you" and sit down. And that's when you turn the corner. I'm old. My wife says, "It's a nice walk, about six miles, what do you say?" and just then I see a taxi and wave and he pulls over and we get in. No more need be said.

I realized I was old when I no longer knew who famous people are anymore—the celebs at the Tonys and Emmys and Grammys and Timmys and Ronnies—Ann Bleecker and Christopher Delaney and Eldridge Fulton and Leonard Mercer—who are these smarmy narcissists with hair piled on their heads and weird eyeglasses? My famous people had mostly died and gone to Halls of Fame. This made me sad and then I realized how liberating it was to know that Madison Mercer's drug troubles and Prince Rector's arrest for DWI and Warren York's wife Sheridan Vandam's allegations of abuse are no concern of mine whatsoever. I'm free to stop reading about them.

Once I knew about stuff and took a cool ironic view of pop culture and now I'm completely out of touch. I'm off the grid, like the Amish, and I feel lighter for it. I've put away the clock and now I enjoy the time.

When John Updike and Philip Roth, the deans of American fiction, died, it dawned on me that my time was past. The tables at the bookstore were full of novels by other people's children—"captivating, heartbreaking, and a tour de force," said the blurbs, but the missing words were "sniveling witless drivel" and "self-important and tone-deaf" and "the sensibility of a concrete slab." I read through the first five pages and wonder why the author bothered. The Humor shelf is shorter than the selection of anchovies at the grocery—nobody under 50 wants to be labeled a "humorist," they want their whimpering to be taken seriously. I don't want to know these writers; I've been avoiding people like them all my life, I hear their voices from across the room and I go outdoors.

And I realized there are ten times more people off the grid than on it. The mainstream is a narrow creek. Getting off the grid is a good move, you gain freedom. Except for baseball and some comedy, I haven't watched TV since I was 40 and I used all that free time to make a life for myself.

And so you become an old fart. Flatulence happens. The muscles of the digestive tract degenerate and metabolism slows and the production of stomach enzymes lightens and your lazier lifestyle allows food to sit in the gut longer, and so I sometimes walk into a room, attempting to hold the gas in, but the tightening of the anal embouchure only produces more articulated farts and a whole string of them sound like a sentence, like "Hope for the best and prepare for the worst" or "If ifs and ands were pots and pans there'd be no trade for tinkers," and this makes my wife collapse in hysteria. (Does she fart? No. She talks more than I do and so the pressure never builds up down below.)

I am a lucky man and before that, I was a lucky child. Luck is not the same as privilege. Privilege is having a chauffeur and luck is when the train comes just as you go through the turnstile and walk across the subway platform just as the train stops and the doors open, which makes your entire day up to that point feel fortuitous, perfectly timed, and you feel blessedness. Having a chauffeur makes you sheepish. In the eighth grade, I was working a power saw in shop class, which was where they stuck boys who couldn't do higher algebra, and I was joking around with a pal, the rotary blade screaming through a 2x6, and Mr. Orville Buehler was horrified by my heedlessness—he could see a prosthetic device in my future—and he ran up and turned off the saw and said, "All you do is talk in class so I'm sending you up to Speech where you can get credit for it" and up from the basement I went to Miss LaVona Person's classroom, a major turning point in my life, where I discovered the sublime pleasure of making people laugh, something my fundamentalist parents had neglected to teach me. In the course of two weeks, thanks to Mr. Buehler, I got set on a path to show business. For most people, education and diligence and discipline are the keys to success, but what opened the door for me was ineptitude at the power saw.

I was lucky to have parents who were crazy about each other, a romance made urgent by wild horses. John met Grace in 1931, the dark Depression, and the courtship went on for five years, Grandma needed Dad on the farm after Grandpa died, and one day, driving a manure wagon towed by a double team of horses that spooked and galloped out of control, Dad almost broke his neck when the wagon crashed, and felt his own mortality and the romance became urgent and four months later she was pregnant and they ran off and got married. This wonderful story was kept secret all their lives, but we could see the tenderness between them.

We were Sanctified Brethren. We didn't go in for jokes and we avoided rhythmic movement for fear it would lead to dancing, which could lead to fornication and we didn't play musical instruments for fear we might display talent, which then might lead to employment in places where liquor is consumed and when we sang hymns it was in slow mournful tones like a fishing village keening for its men lost in a storm, but we worshipped the Book, studied it word for word, and we were storytellers, the one art form Jesus embraced in the parables. And my mother, unlike other Brethren, loved comedians, especially Lucille Ball and Jonathan Winters and Burns & Allen, and laughed hard at jokes, and I inherited this love from her.

I was a bookish boy and decided to be a writer out of admiration for H.L. Mencken ("A historian is an unsuccessful novelist. A philosopher is a blind man in a dark room looking for a black cat that isn't there. A theologian is the man who finds it. A cynic is a man who, when he smells flowers, looks around for a coffin."), which seemed like a cool thing to be. I had 20 aunts, some of whom thought I was very bright and said so. I wrote poems that impressed them.

I was 14 when I made the transition from one-armed carpenter to performing humorist and now I am almost 80, which in itself is remarkable. I chain-smoked for 20 years and drove with careless abandon, no seat belt, sometimes after a couple martinis and a snootful of red wine, and my main exercise was walking fast in airports and lifting the roller bag into the overhead so by rights I should be in the Pulmonary Unit with an oxygen tube up my nose and instead here I am, a free man smelling the coffee as it brews, and remembering a song I used to sing on the radio.

Smells so lovely when you pour it,
You will want to drink a quart
Of coffee.
It's delicious all alone, it's
Also good with doughnuts,
Fresh coffee.
Coffee helps you do your duty
In pursuit of truth and beauty.
On the prairie or the canyon
It's your favorite companion.

Tea is overrated,
You do better caffeinated with coffee.
Coffee stimulates your urges,
It is served in Lutheran churches,
Keeps the Swedes and the Germans
Awake through the sermons.
Have a pot of it today,
I'm sure you'll say, "That's awfully good coffee."

I went to college when it was dirt cheap and so did not graduate with my feet in concrete blocks of debt, but was free to imagine a big future. I quit an easy and secure job in Academia that I hated and so was free to get a job offer from a brash young radio station where I wound up spending 40 happy years.

In college, I aspired to be a phenomenal intellectual so I wrote hallucinatory verse and dark stories about a lonely inarticulate hitch-hiker with a guitar on his back, leaving one busted romance and heading for another, singing,

I did not go to Harvard, I couldn't make the grade.
All that I have learned I learned by riding freights.
Sorrow was my major and tuition was low cost,
Louise was my professor and she told me to get lost.
I tried to be a writer but everything went wrong.
Once I had a woman, now she's just a song.

He played for drinks in bars along the way and died with no ID so was buried under a cardboard tombstone with MAN written on it and his guitar was given to the bartender's wife who used it for a planter, to grow hydrangeas in. I showed this story to several women who said, "It's so sad" and they set out to cheer me up. So it served a purpose. But eventually I had to earn a living and landed a job in radio working the early morning shift, which I got by virtue of being willing to get up at 4 a.m. M–F. I was the lone applicant. Eventually I learned how to do a radio show—I went back to comedy, which had worked for me in Miss Person's class—people do not want to be made to feel bad first thing in the morning, that's their children's job—so I wrote humorous songs:

> *The engineer was sentenced to death*
> *And he went to the guillotine*
> *But they couldn't get the blade to drop,*
> *Something wrong with the machine.*
> *They decided he'd suffered enough,*
> *Decided to send him to jail.*
> *But he said, "Hey get me some pliers,*
> *I see where the blade got stuck on the rail."*

And heading down the comedy road I stayed in business until I was 75 though I have no actual definable talent: I have the personality of a barber and fans of my show are shocked to meet me and find a tall silent expressionless man and realize that *all those years they had been listening to a Listener.*

My life is full of mistakes: When you're almost 80, what's the point of denial? An old man is free from other people's opinion of him. My wife loves me dearly, my daughter thinks I can do no wrong. I also have a number of friends. Maybe 20 or 24. It's enough. I never trusted compliments and now I trust them even less. Prizes are a hoax, every single last one, and people who flash their awards are only advertising their insecurity.

Major historic mistakes, I look back now and see, occurred with the appearance of the 17-year-cicada. In 1953, at age 11, I first saw

New York City on a trip with my dad, which made a deep impression—it made me status-conscious since I was the only kid in the sixth grade at Sunnyvale School who'd been to Manhattan and gone to the top of the Empire State and stood in the crown of Miss Liberty and this exclusivity thrilled me and it was part of my wanting to be a writer, writing being a major industry in New York, and then wanting to write for *The New Yorker* and I devoted 24 years of my life to this fool's errand of trying to sound like the sophisticated *We* of *Talk of the Town,* which was amusing and somewhat remunerative but utterly misbegotten. As stupidities go, it was like claiming to have a degree from Oxford or be Katharine Hepburn's cousin.

Seventeen years later, in 1970, I went into radio and spent most of my adulthood trying to do shows that were beyond my reach. I loved radio, having grown up listening to it, and tried to re-create what I had loved, and in the process I met some wonderful people, some of whom are friends to this day, but I never did a show that was good enough for me to want to listen to it afterward.

In 1987, I moved to Denmark (dumb) and attempted to be a Dane and speak childish Danish even to people with shelves of English novels and histories and discovered how American I am, finding it unpleasant to live among people who didn't know the hymns of my childhood or who Emerson was or Rod Carew. In 2004, I wrote a book about my left-wing views and thereby alienated half of my audience and most of my family and what good did it accomplish? Nada. And now, in 2021, I write a book about the beauty of getting old. Who am I trying to convince? Myself. No, cicadas have been a trigger for me and I am worrying about 2038, me at age 96, my wife 81, how shall I care for her, can I still amuse her, will climate change force us to live in Sweden, how will we do the daily crossword, is it possible to get major league baseball on Swedish cable?

I never got involved with Lyme disease or hashish or fentanyl and I escaped from the University of Minnesota after a year of grad school and so didn't wind up an unemployed English instructor working temporarily as a dog walker. I successfully dodged the draft and simply didn't report for induction when ordered to and the feds never came after me. You do what you need to do. I switched to comedy, and I had a little success, then a little more, talking about my small town of coffee drinkers, and then Will Jones, the Minneapolis *Tribune* entertainment columnist, wrote a big warm embrace of a story, and Suzanne Weil gave it the Walker Art Center seal of approval and that was the beginning of many good things. This string of good luck persuaded me that God loves me, which is not how it's supposed to work—adversity and suffering are what draw you close to the Lord, not comfort and pleasure, but the lonely hitchhiker got a job in radio and he liked it and felt useful. Years later, I heard that some young Buddhist monks in Nepal were fans of the show and loved my song "Slow Days of Summer," according to their ESL teacher Jennifer who stopped me on Amsterdam Avenue to tell me, in particular, the verse:

I love you, darling,
Waiting alone.
Waiting for you to show,
Wishing you'd call me though
I don't have a phone.

Young monks felt embrothered to the singer waiting for his love to come and I felt honored. Everyone needs to be useful.

Not my house. Someone else's.

I prospered. For a few years I owned a brick manse with a walled backyard you could've held fêtes and galas and formal embassy receptions in, had there been embassies in St. Paul. I bought a palatial flat in Copenhagen suitable for the queen had she been free for lunch. I had four credit cards in my wallet and was fond of Scotch, the Scottish kind made by Scots, and earthy beers and gin made from Icelandic glaciers, and I never met a wine I thought was overpriced, and then I took the plunge into sobriety and didn't look back. But that's all in the past, those buses left a long time ago. I came through the straits of privilege unharmed. Cleansed, in fact.

In 2003, I met a guy at a party who knew the guy who was Robert Altman's lawyer and so one day I went to Mr. Altman's office and pitched a movie and the great director (*M*A*S*H, Nashville, McCabe and Mrs. Miller, The Player*), unbeknownst to me was seriously ill at 78 and big studios were leery of investing in him but he intended to keep working until he dropped and I had an important advantage, some motivated investors, so we made the movie in 2005, the year before he died, and Meryl Streep had never worked with him and jumped at the chance, and the movie came out and got decent reviews—the guy in *Rolling Stone* said it was better than he'd expected it to be—and months later I was eating lunch with friends at the Café Luxembourg on 70th and Broadway when, as I brought a forkful of salad to my mouth, a woman rushed up and bent down and kissed me on the cheek and the whole café took a deep breath. It was Ms. Streep, who'd been eating lunch 30 feet away. Nobody in the café knew me from a bale of hay except the two friends and they were astonished beyond words and still are, 15 years later. Ms. Streep generates light, and when she gives you a smacker, you feel electricity pass through your body. I forget the plot of the movie but I remember the lunch.

Meryl Streep, photo by Jack Mitchell

Life is good. I can agonize with the best of them about the puritanical progressives and the Ayn Rand majority on the U.S. Supreme Court and the Republican embrace of unreality but I still love doing shows at 79 and during intermission the audience stands and we sing, "Mine eyes have seen the glory of the coming of the Lord" and the sopranos take over and I switch to bass and we look over Jordan and see the angels and we ride an old paint and lead an old dan and you are my sunshine and I'll be your baby tonight and all I want is see you laughing in the purple rain, and this makes me deeply happy, and so does writing a book about the joyfulness of aging. It's nothing you look forward to and when you're in it, you know there's only one way out and it may be a rough ride, so love today with your whole heart and leave next week to the actuaries and next month to the economists, and next year to the geologists.

Well-to-do, middle-class, broke,
Whether you doze or are woke,
If you're still alive
At age 65,
Remember this, Jack,
There's no turning back,
You've joined us elderly folk
And you won't get out till you croak
So take sheer delight
In today and tonight
Though you are early baroque.
Delight in the days,
Let each one amaze.
Life is a pig in a poke.
The music, the talk,
The afternoon walk,
Every ding of the clock at the stroke.
Thank God for each breath
And remember that death
Is the punchline of the whole joke.

Patience, 1540, by Sebald Beham

My freshman poli-sci teacher, Asher Christensen, gave a learned lecture on the separation of powers, went to the Faculty Club for lunch, lay down on a couch and died of a heart attack at 57. My best friend Barry Halper took his eye off the road for a minute and crashed into the rear of a stopped school bus and died at 21. I think of the poet Roethke who died at 55 for lack of a drug I take twice daily. *(A lively understandable spirit once entertained you. It will come again. Be still. Wait.)* He grew up in Saginaw, Michigan, a factory town where men like to slide into the bars at 9 a.m. and enjoy a few hours of oblivion. Roethke was a drunk and he also wrote *I knew a woman lovely in her bones, when small birds sighed she would sigh back at them.* I gave a speech in Saginaw once and afterward the chairman of the speech committee said, "It's so hard to get first-rate speakers to come to Saginaw." I didn't ask what he meant; he sounded like he needed a drink. I quoted Roethke in the speech, the lines *God bless the Ground! I shall walk softly there, and learn by going where I have to go.* Death at 55 is much too soon, so thank you, God, for science.

Tom Keith

My colleague Tom Keith who was in radio with me for 30 years doing sound effects and various voices, especially teenagers and talking dogs and monosyllabic husbands, died at 64 of a pulmonary embolism on a Sunday evening at his home in Woodbury, just felt sick and fell down and died in the ambulance racing to the hospital along a street he had always driven on to Lunds to buy groceries and that was six days after a party after *A Prairie Home Companion*, where someone asked if he had tapes of our early shows together, and he said, "We are buying them up off eBay and destroying them one by one." Then he was dead. This happens more and more. I went to visit Paul Yandell at his home in Nashville, sitting in a wheelchair, tubes in him, and reminisced about our days on tour with his boss Chet Atkins, and I told him to be sure to come see my show at the Ryman in April, and he leaned forward, out of earshot of his wife, and whispered, "The doctor says I won't make it past January." Then he died a few days before Thanksgiving, a fine second guitarist who stuck with Chet like a shadow, gone, taking wonderful stories with him.

Once on a small jet heading west in rough weather over the Rockies, Paul leaned forward and said, "I can see the headline, 'Chet Atkins and Garrison Keillor and Six Others Die in Plane Crash,' and I'd be one of the Others." I said, "Paul, when we die, we're all Others." A little bit of truth.

In 2001, feeling breathless, I found myself a good doctor, my cousin Dan, who listened to my heart and shipped me off to Mayo for open-heart surgery. I was 59. Two uncles died at 59 of the same heart problem—a mitral valve prolapse—that Dr. Orszulak repaired, a procedure that wasn't available for Uncle Bob or Uncle Jim. When my dad lay in a hospital in 1999, the man in the next room was Dr. C. Walton Lillehei, the father of open-heart surgery, also the papa of the pacemaker, which I have too. He died of cancer. Two years later, the operation he pioneered saved my life.

Maybe I have 10 more years. What a gift. A whole decade to enjoy clocks ticking, fresh coffee, a walk in the park, deep-fried cheese curds and chili dogs, singing "Under African Skies" with a tall woman, the pictures on my phone of my wife and our daughter grinning, and the video of the audience singing "It Is Well With My Soul" and the pleasure of writing a twisty sentence that will be the beginning of a column. I sit in a café on Amsterdam Avenue, couples walk past and a long-legged runner in denim shorts who, three feet from me, lets out a burst of methane like the honk of a goose, a feature of New York, beautiful women who express themselves freely and without apology. All along the avenue, people kibitz, chew the fat, schmooze, shoot the breeze, conducting multiple centripetal contrapuntal conversations, and the cops stop for a smoke, the waiter grins as she sets down the bill, which moves me to tip her 40 percent, that smile that says, "Oh, earth, you are too wonderful," which I couldn't say when I was young and cool and now that I'm not, I can and do. Happiness is a close marriage and having work to be done. Others have known this same happiness. Fascinated by the naked female form, Botticelli, Gauguin, and Goya kept knocking out the nudes, despite syphilis, liver dam-age, lead poisoning, and the knowledge that their death would wildly inflate the market value of their work, creating fortunes for the Duke of Earl and other arrogant schlumps and nothing for the artist's heirs. Posthumous prosperity: a rotten deal. But onward they went, spritz-ing the paint, washing the brushes.

Seated Nude Seen from Above,
1888/1889, Paul Gauguin

I want to write a novel about an old man who takes a drug that makes him 26 and he is horrified by youth and being swamped by lustful ambition and hanging out with stupid people and in a suicidal panic he throws himself into the river but is rescued by an old woman in a canoe and her kindness renews his faith in the goodness of humanity and the drug wears off and the next day he's old again and they sit down to a pleasant lunch in the park and a glass of wine and he tells her about his amazing experience and she has him committed to a mental hospital where, oddly, he feels more at home. But first I need to write this book about the glory of getting old. The world needs this book and I seem to be the one to write it. My wife has read parts of it that come later and she says it's good.

1

THE DEADLY PRECIPICE

I recall that my old age began when I was in my late fifties and telling a friend about the polio epidemic when I was sent to my aunt's in the country, a little house with a big garden and an outhouse out back and how I chased a chicken with a long wire hook made from a clothes hanger and caught it and killed it and Aunt Jo cooked it over a woodstove and asked me to say the blessing and I'd never prayed in front of grown-ups before but I did a decent job of it, and the friend I told this to had an odd look of unrecognition in her eyes as if it were a story about the Rutherford B. Hayes administration whereas it was from 1949, the Truman era.

Plucked Clean, 1882, William Michael Harnett

She said, "A polio epidemic?? When did this happen?" I was a museum exhibit and she didn't seem curious to hear more. She excused herself to find other company. I had passed into the realm of agedness. And now I've gone way beyond it. My nephew who was born the day after JFK's assassination is now a grandfather. Wrap your mind around that, if you can.

Actually the aging process began when I was 21 and my girlfriend made fun of my galloping up stairs two at a time and also asked me to please not pee directly into the water in the toilet bowl but onto the side—"You sound like a horse," she said—and so I gave up enthusiasm for dignity, gave up shooting baskets in the driveway and playing hockey on the river and paid more attention to my look and forming a personal style, that of a dissident artist who asks no favors of anyone. She was the girlfriend who invited me to visit her when she babysat at the neighbors' and when their kids went to bed, we watched a movie and there on the sofa amazing things happened. Watching the movie led directly to carnal indulgence just as the elders warned. I was glad to give up innocence. I took to wearing a tweed jacket with elbow patches and tie because it seemed to draw the attention of women, more than if I looked like a migrant farmworker. I told them I was a writer. And in due course I was, writing in English, a language learned from my soft-spoken parents, from the formal prayers of the Brethren and their reading of the King James and their stately hymns, from the talk of uncles who were farmers and salesmen and clerks, from piles of books at the library, the reminiscences of my aunts, the jibber-jabber of school hallways and cafeteria, from radio comedians and the beautifully proportioned poetry of jokes.

Language, however, is not crucial and never has been in matters of romance. A woman is not impressed by a love poem any more than Frost's poem "Birches" made his trees grow taller. Women can read men without a word being said, meanwhile the man's hormones are raging and the sight of a female bosom, especially one half-concealed, turns his brain to raspberry Jell-O. She is in the driver's seat, her foot on the clutch. Before she crossed his path and smiled, he only wanted to go down to the lonely sea and the sky, and all he asked was a tall ship and a star to steer her by, but Suzanne took him down to her place by the river and he touched her perfect body with his mind and instead of the white sail's shaking and a grey dawn breaking, suddenly he was eating breakfast with a lady with a basketball under her nightgown who was nauseated and held him fully responsible for that and all her other troubles.

Next thing he knows, they have four children, which kills off the romance that created them, what with arranging playdates and fixing nutritious meals and driving them to advanced preschools, practicing the religion of American parenting, serving the whims and wishes of the little savages, tolerating their horrific music, spending two decades as indentured servants. The man sees his wife come out of the shower, he puts his hand on her bare shoulder, she says, "Not now." Her way of saying, "Enough out of you. Put it back in your trousers."

I've left out a few details—insane in-laws, evil bosses, demonic neighbors, punitive theology, mind-deadening commutes, a wretched home team that makes you ashamed to show your driver's license ("You're from there??? Loserville?")—but this is the Typical American Male Story, from Adolescence to Erectile Dysfunction. And then one day a young woman in the airport says, "Here, let me help you with that," and takes your roller bag and you realize you're on the downward slope.

I was too busy to think about aging. I wrote a bunch of books, some of which should've been left unfinished, wrote a weekly radio show with a 15-minute monologue, played a cowboy, Lefty, and a detective, Guy Noir. I once sang a duet of "Love's Old Sweet Song" with soprano Renée Fleming. (Imagine Rin Tin Tin singing with Renata Tebaldi.) Several books of mine got good reviews ("amusing yet poignant"). I played Carnegie Hall and Radio City. I became a champion writer of limericks, some of which I've seen in print attributed to Anon. but they're mine, including:

A vegan who lived in Seattle
Avoided fish, fowl, and cattle.
No flesh, blood, or bone
Or vegetables grown
On or near the site of a battle.

Re-creation of Battle of Hastings, Hastings

I sang with orchestras, did lectures, solo shows, benefits for Worthy Organizations For Rich People To Help Poor People Without Being In The Same Room With Them. I had no time to think about aging. My wife told me when I got old. We went to a movie and she said, "Now you can get in on the cheap ticket." It was a revelation. I paid full price but knew something had changed. She had become aware that she was married to a senior citizen and now, whenever I got up in the night, I could hear her voice from deep in the pillows say, "Are you okay?"

Both my grandfathers died at 73. People got old earlier then and felt weary and achy and said so. Their dentures didn't fit, their feet hurt, they were half deaf. My aunts and uncles looked forward to death when they'd be united with the Lord and their loved ones. Heaven would be a family reunion, a happy one, free of worry and care. The cheerfulest aunt was Ruby, who was imprisoned by MS in a wheelchair. Whenever we stopped in to visit her, she had a big smile on her face and we stood around a piano and sang to her and she was thrilled. Mother's dad was a worrier and saw trouble everywhere he looked. His daughters tucked him into a rest home and he rested to death. My grandma Keillor was a farm woman, a widow, who'd raised eight kids on a little dairy farm, and in her old age she kept working until she dropped, she didn't know what else to do.

You learn about oldness from watching people get old. Ruby was thrilled by our visit because she'd been looking forward to it for hours. Grandpa had nothing much wrong with him so he was forced to be a worrier, otherwise he'd have been happy, which would've gone against his Scottish nature.

I raced through my sixties, accepting all invitations, churning out Guy Noir sketches: (*Call me a cynic but nothing clarifies a man's thinking quite like looking down the barrel of a revolver in the hand of a man who is seriously irked and considering homicide and trying to remember how to make it aggravated manslaughter instead.*) Seventy hung in the far distance like Mount Kilimanjaro and then (SCREEEEEEEEEEECH) suddenly there I was. It hit me hard at first. Just as Kilimanjaro would if you crash-landed. I flew to New York and when the flight attendant said, "If New York is your final destination," it gave me the willies, thinking of winding up under a stone in a cemetery in Queens, and when she said, "We will be on the ground shortly." I didn't want to be "on the ground"—walking across the ground, yes, but not "on the ground" with uniformed men performing CPR there at Gate C28 at LaGuardia and a crowd of onlookers thinking, "Well, the guy was seventy, after all."

I did a 70th birthday concert with the New York Philharmonic and sang a bunch of my sonnets, one a prayer, five love sonnets, one about cunnilingus. I doubt that anyone had ever sung a sonnet about oral sex at Lincoln Center before, but when you're 70, you've got to work harder to get people's attention.

In the morning she awoke, my dear lover,
in bed, on her back, buck naked,
and I crept under the cotton sky and over
a hill with tufts of sea grass and snaked
my way into a ravine and there found
a delicate creature trembling with sensation
a pink anemone that I touched and (whoa) the sound
of a soprano singing Italian, German, and Croatian
simultaneously, and so I put my tongue
to it and tasted caviar and Cabernet,
and from above was softly sung
a Puccini aria by Billie Holiday
so prettily and then a shudder and a sigh,
and we lay quietly, the opera star and I.

It's the Sonnet Cunnilingus that Shakespeare wanted to write
and could not for fear of what Elizabeth might think or the Earl
of Southampton, but now I have sung it at Lincoln Center with an
entire string section behind me, and I see wonderment in the audience, ladies thinking, "Is this what I think it is?" and it's wonderful
to cause wonderment, especially in a worldly Manhattan crowd that
has seen everything twice, but not this. Until now. It doesn't rank
with "My love is like a red, red rose" or "Give me my Romeo, and
when he shall die, take him and cut him out in little stars, and he
will make the face of heaven so fine that all the world will be in
love with night" or even "Be-bop-a-lula, she's my baby," but it was
a good move for a man known for rural nostalgia to come out in
favor of eroticism. Now and then, people approach me in New York
and after some small talk they say, "I saw your concert with the New
York Philharmonic" and I see admiration in their eyes. I'm sure they
look at Yo-Yo Ma the same way but he had to put in years of hard

work perfecting his ear and technique and all I had to do was write an erotic poem.

William Shakespeare, 1856, John Chester Buttre

Being old does not qualify me as an object of pity. I am married to an adventurous woman who is fond of me and is able to read instruction manuals. When I am tempted to throw the new printer over the parapet to hear it crash on the pavement below, I have her, a rational reader of instructions. She raised our daughter while I was flitting about the country doing shows and amusing myself. She has forgiven me for things I cannot yet forgive myself for. She looked after me when I suffered a stroke. She mostly enjoys my company, a quiet guy who doesn't try to impress her by explaining algorithms or opining on world affairs. There is a self-editing mechanism in me; I don't even talk about how it was when I was young—young, schmung, I was full of grief, I got over it. She beats me at Scrabble because she knows rare words like *xi* and *aeio*, which is Egyptian for something or Greek. She is braver than I and dared to be moneyless in New York and I did not. I am a better sleeper. We still enjoy activities of a naked nature, and my liver and pancreas, kidneys, spleen, ducts, valves, the islets of Langerhans, all are doing their jobs whatever those might be. Even on my worst days, when regret and remorse hang on me like wet bath towels, I remind myself that I achieved old age through luck; virtue was not a factor.

As a child, I rode standing up in the front seat next to Daddy as he drove 75 mph across North Dakota. When I was 19, I was a camp counselor and led three canoes of nine 14-year-olds across an enormous northern Minnesota lake in a thunderstorm, the sky dark purple, bolts of lightning, me an English major with no lifesaving training, canoes with no life jackets, and we reached the opposite shore. No lives were lost, it didn't get in the papers, my life wasn't shattered. I once locked myself out of a rental cabin in Utah while naked in a hot tub and walked around the neighborhood ringing doorbells with only a blue plastic sheet from the woodpile for a covering and nobody called the cops. When I was 42, I went canoeing in the Apostle Islands on Lake Superior and paddled into a watery cavern under Devils Island, ventured deep into it because it was fascinating, a natural light show of reflections between water and the quartz and mica in the low ceiling. I had to crouch down low to get in and eventually it was too low and I turned around and paddled out and a minute later, the wake of an ore boat a mile away came crashing into the cave and my canoe rose and fell on the big waves. That was as close to death as I'd ever come, one minute away. Had I stayed in the cave another minute, *Lake Wobegon Days* would've been a posthumous book. It was my big opportunity to be a notable tragedy.

I was reluctant to retire for fear it would make me old. When I was 74, I did a 26-city tour just to show I could still walk around on stage talking and not fall down. My 75th was terrifying, but I put on a party and a crowd of geezers and geezerettes dined on aged beef and heirloom tomatoes with a dry but experienced Pinot Noir and I received dumb birthday cards ("Welcome to the Incontinence Hotline ... Can you hold, please?") and a T-shirt ("My Goal Is To Live Forever. So Far, So Good.") and my birthday cake was brought in, a major conflagration that set off smoke alarms and terrified small children, and the crowd sang to me in their horrible ruined voices and said I looked good, even though I knew otherwise. I had eyebrows the size of fruit bats and my throat wobbled when I spoke and the skin was crinkly on the inside of my upper arms.

A month later, I went whooshing past my life expectancy of 77.6, and I started throwing away boxes of old manuscripts to spare my darling from having to deal with them whenever she planted me in the Happy Memory Unit. And then, a month later, I was 79, standing at the pearly gate, waiting to be 80.

It is a righteous moment in life. You lose your grip and drop things. You shrink. You struggle to stand up from a chair and your loved ones hold their breath and the ones who know CPR review the procedure in their minds. You take a few steps and someone says, "Can I get something for you?" She is your daughter, she saw you cross a street yesterday into oncoming traffic and you broke into a gallop but there was no gallop available, you ran like a terrified duck. And now she reaches out to you as you take tentative steps across the living room carpet. She sees the wrinkle in the rug where the lamp cord is buried and she imagines you tripping on it and falling. She thinks, *Please don't fall. Do. Not. Fall.* People your age are falling like dominoes, veterans of wars, former football stars, ballet dancers,

Olympic gymnasts, and many of them land on their heads and then can't remember who is president or why.

Terrible things can happen. You go for a walk one morning and a thin patch of ice might bring you down, twisting, waving your arms, squealing, and you enter a world of pain and an odyssey from Mayo to Cleveland Chiropractic to Chicago Shiatsu to Sister Faith Coomer at Holiness Baptist in Luttrell, Tennessee, and a mindfulness class in Santa Fe where a woman named Maple shows you how to exhale all your stress and anxiety, except anxiety isn't your problem, you've broken something.

Memory loss is here. Now. You turn to a friend you've known since childhood and say, "I'm sorry but what is your name?" It happens. My trick for remembering my doctor's name is to think *dentistry*, which involves the teeth and what do you do with teeth? You gnash them. My doctor is Tom Nash. The other day, sitting on the throne, I saw that the toilet paper dispenser was empty, no extra rolls of tissue in sight, and the Chief Provisioner was off on her daily walk, and so I hiked around the apartment, pants at half-mast, looking for the goods. I've lived here for 20 years so this is ridiculous, opening cupboards, looking in drawers, hoping she does not walk in and see me the noted author in this delicate moment. As Mencken could have said but did not, "An author is a man who, in the absence of toilet tissue, is forced to use his own manuscript and regrets that he wrote on such stiff paper."

It's a perilous age, the old one. You're no longer active tense, you're the past, you're in a subjunctive mood, a non sequitur with legs. Photography becomes your enemy. My sweet grandma Keillor looks angry in all the pictures we have of her because she hated having her picture taken so she glared at her relatives when they got their cameras out because she'd seen the results and so she left behind evidence of ferocity though actually she was sweet and loving. My

Brethren upbringing did not encourage personal pleasure and so my facial muscles are unable to form a smile, only a grimace, so in photographs, surrounded by happy family, I look like the borderline personality disordered uncle they've come to visit at the Home. People look at the picture and think, "Cosmetic surgery has come a long way, you don't have to come out looking like an endangered lemur."

My mother lived to be 97, the last of her generation, and her great triumph toward the end was to overcome her lifetime habits of frugality and take full pleasure in an extravagant first-class flight to London and a week on a luxury train across Scotland with five young relatives, the gift of her wayward author son, and after a brief ritual of refusal, she accepted and he told the travel agent to spare no expense and Mother, though in her nineties and wheelchair-bound, a lifelong mender, canner of vegetables, rag rug weaver, bargain shopper, ate well and enjoyed the scenery from her train bedroom and drank her share of some fine wines. She did it for the sake of the young relatives. It was easy for the author son, it was a heroic leap for the canner and coupon clipper to be a wealthy duchess on an excursion, and she carried off the performance very well and the young ones got to see her as a grande dame.

Ships in Distress off a Rocky Coast, 1667, Ludolf Backhuysen

Life is a series of sinking ships, and in the end, you wash ashore on a desert island, but it isn't deserted. There is a handsome woman under the coconut tree, and I marry her and now it isn't an island anymore, it's a nation. That's the happy ending to my life story and I live it every day.

The island I met her on in 1992 was Manhattan, and we moved in together and three years later married, and two years later our daughter was born, and for all these years, my wife has loved Central Park, the island of green within the island, where she likes to run, among fiftyish men in fear of mortality and women out to get a half-million advance on a book ("penetrating, provocative, unflinching, nuanced, dazzling") about their quest for identity. My wife runs. I walk and when she's out of sight, I sit. Women walk by with designer dogs, coiffed at a salon, accessorized. Huskies pull the sled that brings the vaccine to the Arctic village, German shepherds guard the perimeter of the air base and rip the throats of enemy spies attempting to steal nuclear secrets. Golden retrievers locate lost children. Border collies carry crucial messages through a snowstorm to a distant outpost. Manhattan dogs tend to be pillows who poop.

I sit and watch the parade and then I get up and walk. At 81st, where Teddy Roosevelt sits on his horse defending the Natural History museum, I go down into the subway, hang on to the overhead bar, feet nicely spread, as we rumble south, six complete strangers within a few inches of me, everyone in his or her own space, avoiding eye contact, thinking our own thoughts. I once saw John Updike on a downtown C train, the good gray man of letters grinning at the life around him, and once on the same train I saw the master trumpeter Wynton Marsalis. Nobody bothered either one of them and they rode along with us commoners. Both times, I tried not to stare.

"On any person who desires such queer prizes, New York will bestow the gift of loneliness and the gift of privacy," said E.B. White. "No one should come to New York to live unless he is willing to be lucky." I don't belong here but then neither do most of the others. It's a good city for the elderly because you don't need a car, nobody's in a hurry because it wouldn't matter if you were. No alleys so everything happens out in the open, goods are trucked in, garbage is trucked away, every street is a loading dock with flower boxes, and there's something of interest every hundred feet or so.

One day, when I'm planted in the Home for the Happily Medicated, my mind will revisit this city again and again. From Trinity church-yard where lies Mr. Hamilton, who got not one thin dime from the musical he gave his name to, through the Village where brilliant and dedicated but bewildered people once lived in garrets on very little money, to Grand Central with its starry ceiling and the Oyster Bar, the stone lions of the Public Library, a block away from 25 West 43rd Street, an address once known to all young writers who sent our stuff there in hopes of *The New Yorker* publishing it. On 44th is the Algonquin Hotel where I once had lunch with the editor William Shawn. He was sitting alone at a table for two and I walked over to say hello and he offered me the other chair though I'm sure he pre-ferred to be alone. I ordered a cheeseburger and fries and he ordered dry toast and a glass of hot water. When I left him, I walked out to see Eudora Welty waiting for a cab. A frail but elegant woman to the cab-driver, and to me a Famous Living Author. I'll sit in the Home and look back on the greenmarkets with the goods on wooden pallets, the skateboarders swooping past, the cheese department at Zabar's where you gain weight with every deep breath you take, and the schist out-croppings in Central Park. My family forbade dirty talk and so the word "schist" is an old favorite of mine.

It's a simple life, no Algonquin lunches anymore, just breakfast with Jenny, outdoors if possible. Work. More work. The hourlong nap. Perhaps an afternoon walk, to postpone the wheelchair. A luxu-rious unrushed phone conversation. Letter-writing, pen on paper. I've saved six unread novels by my hero John Updike and four by Philip Roth and now I am starting in on them. Horace awaits, Virgil, Ovid.

We got onto a two-meal-a-day regimen, light breakfast, big late lunch. Sometimes we drive up to her family's old cottage on the Connecticut River so she can weed the flower beds and plant things and walk along country roads and relive memories of her solemn grandpa and chatty grandma and her lunatic uncle and the wildly gay cousin Howard who lived with various boyfriends next door. The place is dear to her and therefore dear to me. I sit on the porch and work.

I have work in progress along several fronts and some mornings I rise with clear ideas delivered overnight, maybe a fresh joke, maybe a surgical cut of a tumorous passage. I look at the newspaper but only briefly and if the headline is More Of The Same, I read no further. I don't read the Opinion pages. The anguish of pundits is of no use to me whatsoever. I am an old man in love. This is the natural state of things: anguish is for your thirties, not your seventies.

Serenity is freely available. I sit and wait and it arrives. Anxiety is for other people: you google "infectious disease" and you'll be offered 1,437,893 things to think about. I am free of the world and it is free of me. I am not a worrier. I saw a young woman lying stark naked in Central Park last summer and of course I didn't stare but noticed an older man, fully dressed, sitting near her so I figured he was with her and if she needed me she could've yelled, which she did not do, so I didn't walk over and make inquiries, I walked on. At one time, this would've aroused my curiosity, but no more. St. Paul writes about the old self and the new self, the old proud self that refuses to yield to cars trying to merge onto the freeway and the new self full of kindly patience, and it strikes me now, sitting in the park, that the new self arrives when you're old enough to slough off the old self. My old self wrote a wicked satire of Dylan's "Forever Young," a dumb song, and my new self decided not to sing it on the radio because it would only irk his fans and what good would that accomplish? I was 72 at the time. Old age is a spiritual state, you see you're not the center of the universe, not even the center of south Minneapolis. I have a friend who switched from atheism to agnosticism so he could pray for his granddaughter who is schizophrenic, living in a bad dream. He resisted faith as long as he could but now he's 85 and he unlocks the door to the mystery, not wide open but the bolt is withdrawn. Maybe an angel will look in on him to see what is needed.

In college, I acquired an attitude and now I am done with attitude; I don't care for coffee cups with smartass sayings on them. A woman talks to me at a party while wearing a black T-shirt ("I look like I'm listening but actually I'm waiting for someone else") and holding a coffee cup ("Smart Girl: is that a problem?") and I am perfectly friendly and pretend not to read English, she gets no rise out of me. I converse with teenagers and obscenities flutter like autumn leaves and I do not flinch. The teenagers wear earbuds, the music turned up loud, it sounds like cockroaches eating their brain cells. I smile a paternal smile. We had stupidity in my time too and I participated in it gladly but only up to a point. No acid, no reefer or mind-altering substances. I enjoyed my mind, full of memories and ideas. I'd had enough mysticism with the Brethren.

Now I'm over it. Life itself is good enough. Big things don't bother me, little things make me intensely happy. My frequent-flyer credit card makes me happy just like Green Stamps made my mother happy, just like Wordsworth loved daffodils or Mary Oliver loved wild geese and grasshoppers, the idea of Saving Money While You Spend, earning mileage from the purchase of a sofa so you can fly to Minnesota, it's a miracle, no other way to look at it.

I have a Coke in a skinny glass packed with ice, the coldest Coke ever, and with it a bowl of guacamole with thin slices of radish and onion, cilantro, and the combination of ice-cold soda and guacamole makes me feel 17. This happens often, also when I write a good limerick. *A marketing genius named Pitts could sell Kool-Aid at the Ritz and once for Hanukkah he sold a harmonica to the great Vladimir Horowitz.* The Dairy Queen is as great a pleasure now as when I was 13 and went to the one on 38th Street in Minneapolis on Sunday night before 7 o'clock gospel meeting where the preacher laid out a vision of an eternity of fiery torment in the smoking pits of hell, an eternity of unbearable torment, a scary thought though difficult to grasp. Dairy Queen was a reminder of the goodness of life. I don't need gourmet ice cream. A DQ Butterfinger Blizzard tells me that God loves us.

Jenny enters the room and stops behind me and puts her hand on my shoulder. No words are spoken. A silent touch. I don't recall her doing this back when I was Prince of the Realm and the admiring mail came in canvas sacks and Pooh-bahs and Potentates took numbers to wait in line, but this small silent gesture of hers moves me now. Even after 30 years, she wants me to know she is grateful for my presence. I am not a decorative husband from IKEA, reupholstered when needed. I am the man she loves. She puts her hand on my shoulder to say, This is you and therefore this must be me. (Or maybe she's checking my pulse.)

We can be distant in one room together and then I think of a passionate night in a lodge at the Grand Canyon after which we stepped out on the balcony and looked into the floodlit canyon, which ever since has held erotic significance for me, as does Yellowstone and Old Faithful and Boston and New York and Rome and her parents'

house on Rice Street in Anoka. We necked once in their basement and they sat up above us, reading, and didn't call down to ask if we'd like some brownies.

An old man takes pleasure from the ordinary. Twenty years ago, I took my little girl to visit my dad as he lay dying at home in the downstairs bedroom that had been my room when I was 17 and declaring independence, smoking Pall Malls, reading Hemingway and Ferlinghetti and Ginsberg, leaving the books out where he could see them. She was three and he was delighted to see her. He moved his foot under the blanket and she reached for it and he moved it away and she grabbed again and missed and again and again and then she got him in hand, which delighted her. They played Toe Tag for 10 or 15 minutes. He was 88. He and I were not capable of reconciliation but less is more when you're 88 and I had given him one more granddaughter and it was enough.

I talk to my niece in L.A. who said her new apartment was in disarray, and the word struck me, *disarray*, so elegant, an improvement over "clutter," which makes confusion sound trashy. My niece agrees. "It's what I do," she says, "I bring glamor to confusion." I felt the same uplift once when a hotel clerk said, "Let us know if there's anything we can do to enhance your stay." "Enhance" is a lovely word, seldom heard in conversation. I pray that I have enhanced the stay of some people.

Disarray is the normal state of things, no matter how you try to maintain order. My underwear drawer is a model for all, people ask to take pictures of it, but my mind is churning, trying to recall Newton's Laws, the Ten Commandments, the lineup of the 1955 Minneapolis Lakers, the seven vices, the seven types of ambiguity. Years ago, the Swiss psychiatrist Elisabeth Kübler-Ross came up with the five stages of grief—denial, anger, bargaining, depression, and acceptance, and because she was Swiss, people believed it, though what Heidi and goat-herding and alpenhorns and chard have to do with death and grief, I honestly don't know, but her book was a big hit and the death rate zoomed, just because there was now an orderly process to it, and many healthy old people went sliding down the Kübler-Ross slope, who maybe wouldn't have died if she'd been a Florida RN named Nancy Anderson.

There are five stages of old age, too, but nobody pays any attention because they were developed by her sister Elena who was a Swiss podiatrist and changed her name to Elaine Cooper, and giving up that umlaut cost her millions in royalties. If I were Gårrison Kéillør I would've gone far.

The five stages of aging are: nameless dread, the crisis of bad news, self-pity and disgust, a revelatory experience, and then contentment and maybe even happiness. The stages are not consecutive, and I go back and forth between one and five with a few instances of two.

Joseph Telling His Dreams, 1638, Rembrandt van Rijn

And the Five Stages leaves out a good deal, such as debility, dental (and mental) decay, denial of decline, and also dreams. Old age provides a rich and adventurous dream life, which they don't tell you about in those aging books about retaining a youthful outlook (which is hogwash, of course—why revisit ignorance and naiveté?).

After I achieved serenity (or it achieved me), I went sailing off on uncharted waters to exotic places, a vast improvement over the tepid puny dreams of my working years. I enjoyed epic dreams with elaborate storylines I never could have imagined on my own.

One night I boarded an open-cockpit glider towed by another glider towed by a passenger plane and we flew up into the clouds and over a mountain range and landed in a village in Slovenia. I've never been to Slovenia but in the dream I walked through crowds of Slovenians all chattering freely, which I understood intuitively, it was all very chummy and sympatico, and we toured grand estates with terraced gardens and fountains, sat in an outdoor restaurant, and there met my friend Helen Schneyer for a great deal of feasting and a man gave a speech about one thing and another, which I harkened to carefully, and then we boarded our glider and took off through dense fog and up into the sky. When I awoke I could see I was in my bedroom but still had the sensation of motion, could feel the wind in my face, and so it was with trepidation that I got out of bed. This sort of dream never came to me back when I was a working stiff.

I had a dream in which I was the captain of a four-masted schooner, manning the helm, tossing out nautical commands I'd never heard before, commanding a crew of old salts as we plowed through the waves toward port. My brother, who was a real sailor, was in the dream and he watched me with great admiration. Once I dreamed I was driving a Farmall tractor up steep roads through western forests, towing a wagonload of logs. I played trombone in the marching band at a Notre Dame football game at which the players walk into the locker room and touch the statue of a naked maiden for a good luck, I was hiking in the Grand Canyon, I was a parking lot attendant sitting in a shack and listening to the "Sanctus" from Fauré's *Requiem*, I was driving across Minnesota with a carful of silent friends, familiar old faces and not a word spoken. I had a long dream about Chet Atkins who flew his plane over his vast wheat farm in North Dakota, landing on dirt roads, inspecting the crop, then flying home. Nothing was said about music. I had comic dreams like the one about Bob (Big Old Banjoist) Boynton who ran for governor of Minnesota by singing "My Home's Across The Blue Ridge Mountains" and other bluegrass classics and who once, to dispel rumors, invited the press to watch him make love to his young wife. He was not elected but he didn't care.

Mostly the characters in my dreams were strangers but once daughter Maia and Jenny and I swam at a lake in the desert, floating on rafts. I had a very clear dream of my father, standing in the front yard of my house in St. Paul, watching a storm approach, raising an umbrella as torrents of rain fell, happy as could be. I did a Lake Wobegon monologue and noticed in the audience Brother Frank B. Tomkinson, the preacher at whose gospel service I came forward to accept the Lord as my Savior when I was 14 and he was listening intently as the monologue tiptoed on the edge of adultery and I had to bring it back from the edge. And then, for a change of pace, a classic horror story: a jilted former lover comes at night to a man's home and asks to spend the night. She is beautiful and elegant and friendly. His wife and daughter are fearful, but he invites her in and shows her to the guest room. They walk down a long dark hallway and she comes after him with a knife. His wife and daughter flee to their rooms, screaming. The women chases him up the stairs and he fights her off, throwing lamps and heavy furniture at her and she falls and he kills her with a stone statue. She lies dead, aged, horrible, and he stands looking at her and she rises from the dead, beautiful again, and I awoke. One night I attended the funeral of a friend and although he was Jewish, we sang "Silent Night" and "Joy To The World," as the rabbi stood silently by, and also "Bye Bye, Love," and then I delivered a eulogy in Yiddish. It just flowed out of me. The dead man was so astonished, he poked his head up out of the coffin.

My dream life made me feel I was leading two separate lives, a calm productive daytime and a wild nocturnal one. I come from cautious people and I was a steady good worker for 50 years and now, as a reward, I get to enjoy grandeur and flamboyance and bold fearless experiences in faraway lands.

Why would I bother to fly to Europe? One of these nights I'll probably wind up in Copenhagen having lunch with the queen. My dream life is so wonderful that, for the first time in my life, I look forward to bedtime for a reason other than physical proximity to someone who may have the same idea I do, and I lay my head on the pillow prepared for excitement, and this leads me to imagine death as a dream and not fear the prospect of it. My dad felt heaven would be a family reunion at which he'd see his loved ones as they were in their heyday. I doubt this is true but we shall see. Or if the atheists have the inside dope, we won't. It isn't for me to say. Meanwhile, if you'll excuse me, I'm heading for bed.

2

RULES OF THE GAME

I'm an honest writer, not an inspirational speaker or a sales agent for a seniors condo complex, and believe me when I say: old age is a heroic role you've been preparing for for decades and now comes the easy part: walking tall, exemplifying wisdom and maturity while maintaining humility while retaining the right to freedom of expression and that includes talking to yourself, and despite your eccentricities and crotchets, being beloved. Belovedness is the point of it all. Why would you want anything less? If you are very very old, of course there are no rules, and you can probably get away with homicide if you choose a truly despicable person to poison and you have a doctor who will testify to your mental instability, but anyway here are some helpful suggestions.

Old man writing in a book, angel looking over
his shoulder, after Guido Reni(?)

1. Clean up your act. If you have a beard, shave: skip the Old Testament prophetic look, it gets raggedy fast and people avoid you for fear you'll break into incantations. A beard is no great accomplishment; rejoin the herd. No ponytails: your hair gets thin and you look like a clown with a string coming out of his head. Short clipped hair, natural color, clean-shaven. If you choose an unnatural color, go for black or red, not blond. Trim your nasal hair and ear hair: tufts of underbrush make you look like a demented hermit and raise questions about personal hygiene and toileting habits and make people think about calling a social worker and arrange for Assisted Living and by "Assisted" they mean Supervised. Keep yourself neat. Be appropriate.

Gluttony, from *The Vices*, 1552, Heinrich Aldegrever

2. Less is More. Appreciate what you have. Jesus said so and so did Buddha and Emily Dickinson and Buster Keaton. This is the great lesson of old age. Give up wanting the monumental, the dream home, the trophy husband, the hit show, the Medal of Honor, the Pulitzer Prize for Parody, No. 1 on the list of American Influencers, a close genuine working relationship with Russell Sheridan Thomas. Accept the Good Enough. Love your mediocre grandkids along with the geniuses. Want less, then want even less than that. Jesus said, "Think not what ye shall eat or what ye shall drink. Ask your wife." And so I content myself with a kale salad and a glass of cold

tap water out of the faucet and content leads to contentedness, just as Buddha said. Mysterious, but it really works.

3. Regret is not so interesting. You did it, it was dumb, you wish you hadn't, time to move on and hope the people you did it to do too. So often the confession of sins turns to delusions of grandeur and pride in one's malefaction and a bout of self-abnegation and groveling and flagellation, and people are helpless to stop you and it's very boring. I could list 20 of my regrets, which would only tempt me to list the other 30 but they're not interesting and that's enough about that.

4. Remember where you're from, especially as you try to put your origins in the past. I was in Paris one January on a bitterly cold day, sitting in a bistro, La Ponpon, packed with emaciated young people all dressed in black and elderly communists with enormous eyebrows and embittered poets writing in tiny black notebooks, everybody chain-smoking Gauloises and drinking vials of acidic black coffee and tumblers of absinthe, and a skinny woman across the table from me, reading Albert Camus in French, stared at me and finally asked, "Where are you from?" and I said, "New York" and she said, "No, you're not. You're from Anoka. I'm from St. Cloud. My grandma's from Anoka. She said your people were rather aloof." You can get away from home but you're still who you are.

5. Avoid the adorable, cuteness of all kinds, décor (or people or places or ideas) that try too hard to be charming. It'll be assumed that you, as an elderly person, adore the adorable. Don't. Just walk away and look for what's real. Don't be charming yourself unless you're in the cast of a musical and being paid union scale.

6. Having old friends you've known forever can be a pleasure worth getting old for but it can also lead into long conversations about our health care system that make you dizzy, and honestly I'm not complaining, I'm as fascinated by back pain and varicose veins as the next guy, but it's a pleasure to meet Sarah who majored in physics and went into dance and now, at 23, is a stage manager, or Aidan for whom the numerals 9/11 have no particular significance and who's doing well in podcasting but wants to captain a fishing boat. My friends Bill and Bob, whom I've known since we were in single digits, all go together like peas and carrots and our lunch talk goes in all directions at once, which is pure pleasure, but Sarah and Aidan are the World To Come and listening to them makes me nostalgic for when I was too. I hope they do well, whatever that means in the future.

7. Maintain old standards that are meaningful to you and don't bend with the wind. If you know the subject, pass on your knowledge, no apology. If you want to bow your head and thank the Lord for the burger and fries, do it, no matter if others think it's bizarre. If you believe in playing Scrabble by the rules and not relaxing them as a concession to hobbyists, stand by it. If you don't tolerate casual obscenities in polite conversation, say, "Could you please say *fuck* about half as often as you do? Thank you." My role in social situations is to provide punchlines, and sometimes I sit in silence through a long conversation about cancer or leprosy, waiting for my chance, which irritates some people, but so be it. I grew up in a family that did not hug. I am not a hugger, but if hugged, I respond and don't flinch. My wife is a hugger and she comes from a family that when they see each other they throw themselves into a pile on the floor. I don't join them and over the years they've come to accept this. I have certain standards, I put mustard on a hot

dog, ketchup is for the fries. I love Communion at church when we line up in the aisle and John in the organ loft plays a familiar hymn and we file forward singing "It Is Well With My Soul" or "I Am The Bread Of Life"—it's so moving, it more than makes up for the dry crusty sermon. I love riding Amtrak out of Penn Station and up the Hudson River. I like lunch outdoors under a tree with good company, especially in Minnesota, in the Snow Belt, where it is a visceral thrill to sit outdoors in shorts and a T-shirt, the spine is thrilled and the liver and kidneys, the brain is dazed, the testes are planning multitudes of descendants.

8. Enumerate your benefits, beginning with English, this great language that dates back to 1066 when William, Duke of Normandy, crossed the English Channel to meet King Harold and his Anglo-Saxons in the Battle of Hastings where after a good deal of hacking and clubbing Harold took an arrow in his eyeball and his men took to their heels and the Normans seized power in England and enriched Saxon English with words such as "theater" and "beef" and "language" and instead of pig-snout mud-smeared bare-knuckle Saxon words, elegant terms like "manure" and "excrement" and "coitus" and "penis" with which Norman men won the hearts of fair Saxon women. Our side lost the battle but we won the language to which you and I are heirs and don't give yourself airs, it was a language formed between the sheets. My best friends are English speakers. I did a radio show in English for years and it gave me a social life, I'm unable to make friends one-on-one, I have to do it by broadcasting. So many blessings, GPS and seat warmers and sushi and Google and calculators—I struggled in math and my teachers intimated that I would never have a rich full life unless I learned how to multiply fractions and now, if I ever needed to, which I haven't, I have a calculator in a drawer somewhere. I have

been very well tended by various American doctors for the 20 years since I started to fall apart and this benefit, people caring for the life of another, is at the heart and soul of civilization. Soft butter, aerated, doesn't rip your toast apart like the hard bricks of yesteryear and there you stood eating shreds of toast, feeling that life would be full of disappointment. Not so. YouTube came along with Don and Phil or Little Richard or Glenn Gould, an Assembly of God congregation jumping up and down to "Camping In Canaan's Land," the Beatles' "Please Please Me," or Paul Simon doing "You Can Call Me Al" in front of twenty thousand ecstatic Brits in Hyde Park. In my pocket is a phone, cordless, the size of a half slice of toast, with the numbers of my friends and a video of my daughter laughing hysterically on the River Raft ride at the State Fair as she sees a big wave wet her father's pants. We have gourmet beer with "oak flavors" and "breadiness" and "finish," which we didn't have before, and though I don't drink beer, I know it's available if I need breadiness. In school, we learned about Occam's razor, that the simpler theory with fewer assumptions is more likely correct, and therefore it appears that I am a well-blessed man. I pray that I retain the marbles to be cognizant of this until the lights go out. Things could be worse: I could be seeing a proctologist about my prickly prostate that causes persistent priapism and the presiding bishop of the Presbyterian church could be preaching against my depravity and proclivity for prurient promiscuity, but in fact several Presbyterians are praying for me. As a matter of principle and I am privileged.

9. Old age is foreign territory and you should enjoy it as you would if you'd picked up and moved to Paris. Anonymity is what you're looking for so don't act weird, keep your head down, don't make a scene. Hemingway left Oak Park for Paris, to get away from nosy

neighbors who called him Ern and inquired what he was up to as if it were any business of theirs and gassed about William Dean Howells, that arrogant bonehead, and Hem flew the coop and got an apartment near the Pantheon just up the street from James Joyce and bought Joyce a drink one day and suddenly he was in the club, a writer on the forefront. Did they complain about the food, the rude attitude of Proust students, the rain on the plains of Lorraine? No, they were grateful to have escaped the dim minds of Dublin, the joyless hoi polloi of Illinois. You're old, you're a fugitive, an alien, so make the best of it and be an artist. Dostoevsky ran from Russia. Edith Wharton left Lenox, Henry James, D.H. Lawrence, the list of escapees goes on. Leaving home liberates the mind, so does old age, so throw away your memberships and abandon your lawnmower. Dante left Florence, weary of the civil war between the Guelphs and the golfers, the Medicis and the chickadees and he wrote *The Divine Comedy*, which was divine and also rather funny once you get in on the joke, a poet writing convincingly about hell so he could put people he didn't like down there. What a cool idea.

Dante and His Poem, 1465,
Domenico di Michelino. Florence Cathedral

I think of my friend George Plimpton who died at 76. Roy Blount said, "I was astonished that George died. It was so unlike him." He was Exeter and Harvard, and he had an accent that sounded like his tongue was bandaged, but he had beautiful manners and even if you weren't close to George, he made you think you were. He went to Paris in 1952, when America was admired as the savior of Europe and the exchange rate was good and you could rent a room for $15 a month and dine well for a dollar. He and his friends Peter Matthiessen and Donald Hall and Robert Silvers were all there, hanging out in the Café de Tournon, writing, drinking *vin ordinaire*, looking for Hemingway, living proudly in tiny cold fifth-floor walk-ups, being artists, listening to jazz in the gray light of Paris dawn. They were thousands of miles away from anyone they might meet on the street who would ask, "What are you doing these days?" like dogs sniffing your résumé, expecting you to say, "I'm here for a few days and starting medical school in the fall," expecting you to have a reasonable plan for your life. George was 26 years old right up into his seventies and he died. His books *Paper Lion* and *Out of My League* are part of the permanent literature of sports. You can't really mourn a man who got a life as good as the one he had.

This fabulous luxury of non-citizenship afforded to artists is available to us all simply by getting old and living for the significance of today and not running for public office. We are artists of living well and each old life is a creative work, so make yours stand for something. Old grudges are gone, the ancestral feuds of politics are someone else's province. Once I was a Democrat and now, just as Jesus did, I sit and eat and drink with thieves and sinners—in other words, Republicans (or, as He called them, "publicans"). And if our country goes to the dogs, there's always Canada. The national anthem is impossible and the bacon is round, not in strips, and you have five political parties, but Canada is fairly sane because there is no Florida, no Texas, no South.

Old age is about the beauty of immediacy. I make no bucket list. There's nothing I need to do before I die. Each day is sufficient unto itself. Let me go in peace. Take my saddle from the wall, lead my pony from his stall, tie my bones to his back, turn our faces to the west.

Time is the great luxury, not a big house or a beautiful car or a two-week cruise of the Mediterranean—the main prize is the two weeks spent anywhere you are. Salt air is invigorating, which was why the Vanderbilts built their monstrous mansions along the coast but you're not a crook so Missouri or Minnesota will do just fine. Once in the lobby of the Marriott in Rochester, I met the only billionaire I knew personally, in a wheelchair pushed by his wife. They stopped and she and I talked. He was there to see doctors at the Mayo Clinic. I didn't ask how he was, I could see. He didn't have long. He was 89 and what was crucial to him was time, now that he had so little of it. His daughter was flying in to have dinner with him and he was delighted at the prospect.

10. Don't mention your age. Nobody but the TSA agent will ask your age, so just don't put it out there. Past 70, there's no point in keeping score. The psalm says, "So teach us to number our days, that we may apply our hearts unto wisdom" but it doesn't say to wear the number on your sleeve. On the other hand, don't forget your age, don't be like those old ladies who've had so many facelifts that if they have one more, they may start menstruating. It's not good company to be in.

I tell you I'm 79 (DOB 8/7/42, Anoka Maternity Hospital, a big white house on Ferry Street, Anoka, Minn.) because as a reader you have a right to know this was written by a geezer, not as a joke by a teenage girl named Misty from reading *Modern Maturity* magazine, but I don't go around announcing my 79ness and if people look at me (my hair is still brownish) and imagine I'm 68, it's no skin off my nose. I once met some students at the University of Minnesota and told them I'd graduated in 1966, and to them, 1966 was not long after the Civil War, they were dumbfounded that I was still standing upright and respirating without assistance. They were editors of the same literary magazine I edited a century before and I felt a bond with them because the fiction and poetry they published were just as dreadful as what we published, adjectival, subjective, nonverbal, rather aerial, improbable, indescribable, unreadable, but to them I was a corpse who crawled out of a sarcophagus, so nuts to that. I have no need to dumbfound people. I decided not to talk about the past with people who weren't there at the time. I enjoy the company of young people and I ask them about themselves. They're happy to be interviewed, and I learn a few things. It's about them, not about me. It used to be about me and it isn't anymore.

11. Keep occupied. Rise in the morning with stuff to do. Work is a necessity, not just the crossword puzzle or standing in a group of slim silent people with binoculars staring at a whippoorwill. If you're in need of a mission, come join my line of work and be amusing to those you love. Jesus did not say, "Blessed are the elderly for they shall be humorous," but undoubtedly He thought it from time to time. (I mean, He was omniscient, *duh*.) I am God's handiwork, put here on earth to do good works, and comedy is one of them. I walk into a room and fart and my wife shrieks with laughter. I sit down, as dignified as I can be, and this makes her laugh even harder. I lean forward to open my computer and out of me comes a bark, like a sea lion calling its mate, and she screeches. I do my best to make an audience laugh but am reluctant to employ flatulence as a technique. (What would you follow it with? Incontinence?) But this woman is delighted, no doubt about it.

12. Don't fight with younger people, even if you're right, which you probably are. When they say outrageous things, say, "That's very interesting, I'll have to think about it." These people will be writing your obituary, and why give them an excuse to put "contentious" or "embittered" in there or accusations of misogyny or cultural appropriation or lack of inclusivity. If you enjoy dispute, go after your elders if you still have any of sound mind. Poke them in the stomach. They'll be amazed, seeing as everyone else pities them to death, and they will relish combat and it will improve their respiration. And a day later they'll forget the whole thing.

13. Get out of the way. You're old and slow, don't be an obstacle. Marathons discourage elderly entrants because they take days to finish, trailed by emergency vehicles with flashing red lights. Send them to a gym and chain them to a treadmill. I come from a wonderful tribe of pissers and moaners, the Scots, who were oppressed by the English and it brought out the best in them, their love of the nobility of being unjustly persecuted, and now we elderly are oppressed by the young, their insane music, their crude manners and loud voices, their goddamn horseshit profanity, their lazy mindless self-pitying memoirs, their ridiculous politics, their self-mutilation by piercing and tattoos, but this is now their country, not ours. We are visitors so let us get out of their way. We had our chance, we screwed up, and our shift is over. My era of Karen and Joanne and Larry and Carol is over, time for the kids with Mediterranean names like Sofia and Isabella, literary names like Nora, Harper, Scarlett, Zoë, Emma. Bring them in, give them the keys to the castle.

    Old people belong on a screened porch, barefoot, sipping an iced tea, dozing over *Anna Karenina*. Don't bother the young with your outmoded ideas, don't comment on that girl's bikini

bottom with the tiny thread up the crack between the bare but-
tocks and don't stare at her enormous gothic tattoos. Back in my
day, tattoos were worn by the ex-felons who ran the carnival rides
and now they're worn by graduates of Smith and Vassar employed
by the Ford Foundation. Get that? She thinks the pagan tattoos
are totally cool. We're old, we don't think in terms of totality:
"Sort of happy" is as far as we go or "kind of interested," but the
young are totally into what they're into and it's awesome. You
and I never achieved awesomeness. It was in dictionaries back
then but went unused. Awe was what you would feel if the clouds
parted and flights of angels descended with Jesus in their midst,
the radiant brilliance of His holy light: it would be awesome.
Now you might apply the word to a podcast or somebody's hair.
Times have changed so be open-minded. If your daughter pulls
up to McDonald's drive-up window and orders the usual and
hands you yours, take a bite and say "awesome," and see if it
doesn't make the thing taste better.

14. Past a certain age, probably the one you're at now, it's okay to use
the microwave, especially for fish but also for most other things.
Dragging out a grill and lighting charcoal and marinating the
meat in a sauce you made from a recipe in a Craig Claiborne
cookbook is all well and good up to the age of 50, but Craig is long
gone and there's nothing magical about a flame so cut to the chase.
Less time cooking, more time talking. And if you need that second
cocktail, okay. And if you feel like putting on your jammies at nine
o'clock, don't give it a second thought. You are excused.

15. Beware of persons who, in friendly conversation, use terms such as
"multilayered," "skill sets," "dynamics," "productive capacity," and
"disincentivize," and if they try to persuade you to do something,

change the subject and ask about their most recent bowel movement, assuming there was one.

16. Walk carefully. Look where you're going. Stabilize yourself. Don't think about *Graceful,* the goal is *Equilibrium.* Do not be ridiculous. If you're going to suffer serious injury, suffer it by defending a woman against vicious hoodlums or saving a child from a polar bear, not by tripping on a rug. Every rug is your enemy, every doorsill, every stairway is treacherous. This is no time for magical thinking. Young people are watching, hoping you'll take a header. The Rolling Stones know that and that's why they don't roll anymore, they're standing stones, like Stonehenge. Mick Jagger prances very carefully. Bob Dylan still performs but he no longer sings, "I was so much older then, I'm younger than that now," because he is not in the comedy field, not yet, he hopes.

    Google the words *Core Strength* and you'll find exercises, lifts and bridges and extensions, so do them. Work the glutes, do the bird dog. But don't do them where other people can see because the stifled laughter will discourage you.

17. Be grateful for each and every disaster. I skipped into my seventies, intending to go on forever but new management at Minnesota Public Radio threw me out the window for "inappropriate" behavior and that year "inappropriate" was equivalent to membership in the Communist Party and you became a non-person. Everything was canceled, the line went dead. It was a jolt.

    When you're a kid, the thought of public ostracism is painful and if MPR had done it 20 years before, it would've broken my heart, but the beauty of being an old man is that, after the initial pinch, you feel emancipated by the isolation, like the trapdoor opens and all the envious suckups and resentful tailgaters disappear into the void. To be shunned by jerks is no problem whatsoever. You're done with them and you're left with the company of people you actually like. My wife was ferocious in my behalf; she was angry enough for both of us, no need for me to say a word. And when overnight you lose so much of what you worked for, you realize how beautiful is what's left: WORK itself. A writer can't be stifled without his consent. You sit down to a pad of yellow lined paper and a pack of pens and your brain comes to attention.

I wrote a couple novels and a memoir and life reformed itself around the idea of Time Blessed Time. The pandemic intensified the whole learning experience, a year and a half in Corona Prison, no more parties, no more shows, no more dinners in fancy clothes, and what you learn is simple: one can live without snazzy, swanky, ritzy, and slick. Social distancing comes naturally to us old fundamentalists and the mask means I don't need to smile. I like eating a salad and a grilled cheese sandwich with my wife and daughter at the kitchen table. We are a comedy routine. My daughter says, "Make me laugh" so I tell the penguin joke and the talking dog joke and then I whisper the word "diarrhea" and that does the trick. I wouldn't do it if an archbishop were present or Hillary Clinton, but it's just us. The daughter and mother wrangle and I am the harmless old man in the chimney corner. Weeks of isolation, no sense of time, we enjoy our little routines, I think it should become an annual event, a week of national lockdown.

Fortune, 1541, Sebald Beham

18. Be lucky. Luck is crucial. If you took time to plan your life carefully, you'd be 90 by the time you turn 25. Thoreau said, "We
should be blessed if we lived in the present always, and took
advantage of every accident that befell us."

Thanks to the accident of a dog who jumped on my daughter
when she was three and terrified her, we were spared the burden
of dog ownership. She snuggled with me, I was her dog. And I
can sing, which dogs can't. Almost every day, she climbed into her
old man's lap and put her little arms around my neck and melted
my heart like cheese under the broiler and this was the *Hallelujah*
Chorus and the *Water Lilies at Giverny* of parenthood, when she
said, "I love you so much." Thoreau didn't have a daughter to do
that to him. (He claimed that trees did but I doubt it. He was
lacking luck.)

There's not time to be perfect, only adequate. We live in
ignorance and the educated are merely ignorant in realms they're
unaware of, such as the spiritual. There are no prizes for parenting
or husbandry because so much depends on the weather. Do what
needs to be done to improve your chances. Eat more fruit that
contains potassium, which reduces the chance of strokes, which
can turn you into an object of pity. Walk two miles a day. If you
write a hit song, throw it away. Don't be famous and successful,

it's dangerous. Buddy Holly got into that plane in Clear Lake, Iowa, on a snowy night in 1959, and the pilot misread his instruments and flew it into the ground. Buddy was 22. He was cheated of a long life by his own celebrity: the young inexperienced pilot didn't know how to tell a rock star, "I don't think this is a good idea." So Buddy became a legend but who wants to be a legend? Let Achilles be legendary and you be a regular person.

I'm lucky, which is good because I'm not a sunshiny guy, I go around with a fundamentalist face, I can't smile so my gums show, only a thin slice of teeth, so strangers in need of assistance see me and then look around for someone friendlier. Jesus said to help the needy—why did He give me this hostile face? It makes no sense. But I've known charming people with beautiful smiles who were bipolar, which I'm not, just Midwestern. I never went into therapy so I could talk about how emotionally unavailable my dad was; he simply was and so were other dads, it was the Minnesota syndrome. We were all in the same boat.

A dear friend hanged herself in the garage, another put rocks in her pockets and drowned herself, another overdosed on sleeping pills. After you've known people who've suffered depression, you don't use the word casually. All three friends were educated, capable, beautiful, and very funny women, and after you've seen this happen, you don't ever forget it.

19. There is a lot of outrage going on around us, most of it pretty cheap, and why add to the surplus? Count to 10 before you condemn. I come from judgmental people, northerners, who examine a person and give you a grade that sticks and is not easily appealed. I've carried this disapproving gene, the tendency to be a royal pain in the ass, and now, Praise the Lord, it has left me. I am able to read things I mightily disapprove of and set them

aside, and don't feel obliged to be angry. I just click Delete or Unsubscribe and move along. We don't have a sign in the front yard: THIS HOUSE IS OPPOSED TO GENOCIDE. It isn't for fear that we'll be assumed to be genocidal but for fear the neighbors will feel a need to construct a billboard opposing bestiality, torture, genocide, cannibalism, and the mass incarceration of Methodists. Bumper stickers will appear: *We Stop For Deer.* People will petition the school board to forbid the assigned reading of literature that involves cruelty.

20. Be glad that the worst is behind you, which it very likely is, simply because you lack the energy to be as foolish as you might like to be and lead a life of flamboyant debauchery, ingesting heavy-duty drugs, destroying hotel rooms, throwing $400 bottles of cognac out the 15th-floor window. Debauching is tiring, the shouting and trying to think of things to shout that would shock other swine, the nakedness and lewd dancing and bigamy and trigonometry and quadrangles and quintessentials, it wears one out even to think about it, You would need a nap to even debauch a little. And what is the point of minor depravity and dissolution? Pigs don't snack, they go all the way unless they're chicken.

21. Make it clear to your likely survivors that you do not require a big funeral service. You will be elsewhere, not hovering overhead. Tell them you do not want it to be called "A Celebration of Life" because you have already celebrated your own life as best you could and now there should be a few moments of grief and reflection on the precariousness of our situation, and then go have a wonderful evening and be glad it was you in the urn and not them.

22. Enjoy inertia. Sometimes I see a crowd of Harleys parked outside a biker bar and feel like marching in and smashing a bottle against the mirror and yelling, "Which one of you fairies feels like taking on a successful novelist?" But I don't have the energy to do it. I feel similarly when I see people running in the park, some of them almost as old as I, and I think of the cartilage destruction with every pounding step, the hip replacement surgeons who are buying mansions for their children with the fees they pocket from doing 10 and 12 procedures on a hospital assembly line, repairing people who will never be the same again, who will struggle under the harassment of a vicious 24-year-old PT and get on a regimen of painkillers that leaves them unable to recall the *watchfires of a hundred circling camps* verse of the "Battle Hymn of the Republic," and eventually the family meets and votes to pack them off to the Heavenly Waiting Room and a chaise overlooking the flower garden, a flutist and harpist playing "While My Guitar Gently Weeps." I find a bench and sit down, glad not to be part of that story. I don't run but I can still climb stairs unless they're leading up to the blue sky in which case I prefer to stay down here.

23. Pay no heed to someone else's rules, especially if he has numbered them. Numbering is a substitute for rational thinking. The guy is a writer, he's spent his life looking at a blank screen or blank paper, he missed out on actual life—never taught third grade, never was a cop, never worked in an all-night diner—the man lacks experience. He spent his life working in public radio, which is made up of Americans who like to imagine they're British. It is a somber country with aristocratic pretensions where humorless universalists admire each other's clichés and whimsy passes for comedy and anyone who can stand on one foot and whistle is considered quite an original. His advice is less useful than what you'd get out of the gumball machine. Ignore the rules and go to the next chapter when he goes to the Emergency Room. You might enjoy it. (Spoiler: he survives.)

3

A NIGHT IN THE ER

My grandpa Keillor died of hard work at the age of 73 and I avoided work and am feeling lively at 79. There's a lesson there: find an easy life and if you lack brains and talent, make up for it with brazen self-confidence. Family loyalty brought my grandpa down from Canada in 1880. His sister Mary was in Minnesota and her husband, Mr. Hunt, was dying of TB so James Keillor, 20, left his job in the shipyards of Chatham, New Brunswick, where he was known as a gifted woodworker and took the train to Anoka, arriving just in time for the funeral. Mary had three little children with her on the farm and rather than uproot the kids, James became a farmer and a substitute dad to Sadie, Rozel, and Gertie. Years later, I knew Rozel as an old farmer from whom we bought eggs and he spoke of my grandpa as a hero and a saint. James wasn't a farmer but he worked hard and made do. Same with me, I went into radio, which is like marrying a sick man, and I started a live radio variety show of the sort that had perished decades before, done in by television. I knew what not to do and did something else, which seemed to work out and if it didn't, I tried something else, and a loyal staff carried me through the contingencies, a band of women and men who became a family. After James raised Mary's three, he married Dora, who taught in the schoolhouse across the road. She was 20 years younger. He called her "my dear girl" and he carried her in his arms up to bed at night until he was 70 and fathered eight children by her and died when the two youngest were still in high school. He was tall and lean and handsome and had a sweet tenor voice and my dad inherited the handsomeness. James died nine years before I was born and when I was a kid I studied pictures of him and visited his grave north of Anoka along Trott Brook and before I had my heart operation I bought a gravesite about 60 feet east of his.

Jenny has made it clear she will not be planted next to me and that's fine. She is a restless woman, I'm not sure she'd stay in the ground once put there, it'd be like her to arise and go for walks, and she has little fondness for Anoka where her family, four violinists and two pianists, felt odd among us farmers and truckers, and I think she'd prefer to wind up in New York in Central Park. Our daughter could go out late one night with a posthole digger and plant her mother near the playground at 91st, close enough to the roadway to feel the strides of the runners. We've lived peaceably together, thanks to our differences. She is a violinist, dedicated to perfection, to playing in a string section and not standing out as an individual whereas I am a writer for whom getting attention is crucial (whoop whoop). She feels nauseated if she hears someone say, "Her and me went to the store." I don't. Sometimes it's I who says it. She is a devoted reader, a runner, a patron of art galleries and museums, and it makes her very happy, even giddy, to ride the B train to Seventh Avenue and walk into Carnegie Hall or the C to 50th and the Metropolitan Opera House. She is Anoka born but a true New Yorker.

"There is no point in wasting money," she keeps telling me. So our refrigerator is full of tiny plastic bowls holding small portions of leftovers such as would sustain a Chihuahua. Thanks to her, my consumption of double cheeseburgers is at an all-time low; my intake of greens is now close to that of an adult giraffe. She has accused me of wasting laundry soap. She sleeps with two windows open so it's cold when I wake up and I crank up the thermostat and she turns it back down. I ask if the London stock market crashed during the night. No, she says, but you can put on a sweater if you're cold. She says I put too much coffee in the coffeemaker. We are liberals so the coffee is a locally ground free-trade organic coffee, not made by child slave labor, so I don't feel bad about generous portions, but I follow her instructions. She finds a wad of cash in my jeans pocket and says, "What do you need all this money for?" I need it for good luck. I touch a clutch of twenties and feel secure. But I defer to her and she makes the decisions, in return for which I'm relieved of responsibility, in payment for which I do not complain. She is in charge of anxiety.

For my 70th birthday, we took the *Queen Mary 2* across the Atlantic and she worried about the extravagance, but for nine years I have put myself to sleep at night by standing at the rail as the ship slips under the Verrazano Bridge and out to sea toward England so the voyage has more than paid for itself with more than three thousand nights of good sleep. My sweetie lies in bed worrying about COVID variants and about all of her loved ones in turn and I stand at the rail with a glass of champagne and there you have it: life is unfair. She is a restless sleeper, sensitive to heavy breathing. I offer to get up and go to the back bedroom. "No, no, no," she says. "I can't sleep without you here." So I stay. She tries to read herself to sleep but often winds up in serious territory thinking about extinct species and the melting of glaciers and warming of oceans and I get back on the *QM2* and out past Sandy Hook and the band plays "Nearer My God To Thee" and all is well.

It's a simple conservative life. I watch no TV other than the occasional ballgame. I don't know how to operate the remote and change channels now that there are thousands of them so I work instead. I listen to no radio. Radio was a habit of driving and now I'm a pedestrian. I would no sooner wear headphones than I'd wear a feather headdress.

I do as I wish when I feel like doing it and talk to people I wish to talk to. Cousin Ben about strawberry farming. Cousin Dan on aerial gliding. Sister Linda on family history. Friend Patricia on the world of letters. Daughter Malene on life in London. Daughter Maia if I need to know how to work my computer, I FaceTime her and she explains.

I talked on the radio for 40 years so it was a shock one day last summer when my brain clamped shut and I couldn't form a single word. I was about to say something and it wouldn't come out. I was aware of awareness in my brain but it was stunned. This lasted for about two minutes, I stood looking at my wife with a frozen brain. I called the doctor, whose name I then could not recall except it was the name of a car (Ford? Studebaker? Mercury?). His secretary asked for my phone number and when I couldn't recall it, she put me right through to Dr. Nash. I took a cab over to his office and he quizzed me. I've suffered a couple of strokes in the past, light ones, no lasting damage that I'm aware of, but Jenny recalls my thrashing around and temporary dementia, and Dr. Nash, though I was talking normally now and even trying to be funny, wanted me to be tested for a stroke and since it was a Friday afternoon he sent me to the ER, so I canceled everything and went. My wife kissed me goodbye and said, "You remember that Maia was born there at New York Cornell hospital, right?" I did, then.

I spent 24 hours in the Emergency Room. A man who experiences momentary blankness does not go to the head of the line. It was not deluxe. A little alcove in the midst of the dying and the insane and a few drunks the cops had brought in, a purgatory of yelling and moaning and cool professionals in blue scrubs doing what could be done. I lay in my bunk and felt perfectly fine. I waited my turn. It was suppertime but I didn't buzz for someone to bring me supper; this was not a café, it was a place of suffering.

An old lady six feet away, a thin curtain between us, awoke from her drugged state and screamed, "Help me! Help me, someone!" and then "Just let me die! Please!" and though she was dying, she had plenty of volume, and after she repeated her line nine or ten times, someone came and tried to comfort her. An old man on the other side of me lay cursing the help, accusing them of trying to kill him. The ingenious combinations of profanity were impressive. He'd been brought to the ER by the police after he'd been a public nuisance, walking back and forth on the street screaming at people, and now he called 911 to come and rescue him from the doctors.

Terror mixed with pain, 1862, Guillaume-Benjamin-Amand
Duchenne de Boulogne, Adrien Tournachon

The police were quietly amused by this. One of them offered to be the man's guinea pig and take the sedatives to make sure they were not poisonous: "I could use a good muscle relaxant or two," he said. Between the woman and the man, they had my full attention. I lay in the alcove, gurneys coming and going, beepers beeping, the woman yelling, "Somebody come and help me! I just want to die! Help me!" and my crazy neighbor cursing the nurses who had gently taken away his phone. "I need to call my attorney," he yelled. "I'm collecting your names and I'm going to sue each and every one of you for all you're worth and I'm going to wind up owning this hospital and you're going to be strapped in a bed just like I am now," he said, along with a dozen explosive expletives, but slowed down as something in his IV took effect and said something about calling his senator and cutting off public funding, and this last delusion seemed to exhaust him and he was quiet.

My nurse was Yemeni, the neurologist Israeli, the night nurse was Black from Des Moines. Diversity wherever you looked and a great inclusivity of clients. A variety of wretchedness and anxiety, no visitors except me the tourist.

The EEG technician came in at 4 a.m. and began attaching electroencephalograph wires on my scalp, an intricate gizmo. He was from Nepal but I heard it as "Naples." "Beautiful city," I said. "Country," he said. He worked quickly, placing each electrode on my scalp and freezing it with a coolant gun. I said, "It looks as if you've done this before," and he said, "Yes, but each time is like a new experience." This struck me as the funniest thing I'd heard all day. He thought so too.

I asked his name and he said, "You'd only mispronounce it. Call me Bob." "So you like to work under an alias, then?" I said. He said, "With men your age, yes." We were an act, meanwhile he was putting contacts on my scalp, freezing them in with cold air from the gun. I said, "So Nepal—you're Buddhist, right?" "How could you tell?" he said.

He said, "Buddhism is the easiest religion in the world. Hindus have a thousand rules and I never understood Christianity but Buddhism is easy. You just don't hate anybody. Don't be a jerk." And it struck me how few jerks I've encountered in my long long life and the few I knew felt they were acting out of righteousness and I, having grown up among the righteous, had a streak of that as well. As he stuck the wires to my head, I felt I was being shriven of my righteous cruelties, I'd come to the ER to be purified, the Lord had lowered me into the city's depths to smarten me up a little.

It was almost 5 a.m. The dying woman was quiet, the crazy man had been taken away. I was giddy from lack of sleep, like back in college days. I am not now and never was a wise man and I carry my head under my arm like a football so I take rather short views and gain less firsthand knowledge of the world than a grown man should, not enough to make good solid choices, and thus my sketchy romantic past, the passions that evaporated, but I have been lucky several times, one being the lunch at Docks with Jenny Nilsson when I was 50, and now, having a Buddhist humorist freeze wires to my scalp among the dying and insane in their disarray struck me as a moment of some awareness.

It was the valley of the shadow of death and the Lord prepared a table before me and poured oil on my head. I would walk out of here and be better for having come. Jesus said, "Ye shall know the truth and the truth shall set you free" and here in purgatory I'm surrounded by truth and I feel liberated somehow. All around me is a scene of serious suffering that I've floated over all my life like a boy in a balloon and now it is my privilege to witness it. My neighbors have their own stories, each different, but a load of rocks have dropped on them and now they are conjoined in creaturely suffering. I say a prayer for them: *Lord have mercy, God have mercy.* I made my living in the circus, Mr. Wobegon, and I'm awestruck here in purgatory, as I was once hiking the Grand Canyon and once on the *Queen Mary* out in the Atlantic and once flying in Dan's little plane over Wisconsin at night, the glow of each town visible in the cloud cover below and then once on the uptown C train, packed into a car with people on all sides standing within inches of each other and still not touching, avoiding eye contact, and I may've been the only one thinking of Whitman's *I will plant companionship as thick as trees all along the rivers of America, inseparable cities with their arms around each other, with the love of comrades,* lines no poet would think to write anymore. And then there was that night in this same hospital when my daughter was born and I held the tiny naked being in my hands, her dark eyes gazing about, and I left the hospital and in my happy confusion I went south instead of west and didn't recoordinate until Times Square. And now this night. All the sufferers around me, I'm sure I could've put my shoes on and walked out unnoticed but I chose to stay.

Competence presides in the ER, not attitude: you analyze the problem, arrive at a reasoned plan to deal with the problem, and try to describe the process to the patient. And around noon, the neurologist comes to my little alcove and tells me what the high-tech tests have shown, that I'd only suffered a brain seizure, no lasting stupefaction or systematic imbecilic occlusion.

This is a large event to a near-80 man, a demi-octogenarian. I remember a time I wanted to see my name on the best-seller list (and be cool about it) and draw sell-out crowds and some ticket scalpers out on the sidewalk, be invited onto TV talk shows, attend celebrity events in an Italian tuxedo and mingle with other tuxedos and think to myself, "I'm from Anoka, Minnesota, the land of slow talkers, and I'm representing Billy and Corinne and Sherry and John and the other kids on my bus route, and now I'm backstage at Carnegie Hall and when those kids see this show on CBS, they'll say, 'I know Gary and there he is with Bob Hope, Frank Sinatra, Ray Charles, Marilyn Horne, Tommy Tune, Willie Nelson, Rosemary Clooney, Leonard Bernstein, and Walter Cronkite,' and I look as good in my tux is as they do in theirs." But that's over, thank you, Lord. It was fun, no regret, and now the ambition hormone has disincentivized and I am planted in a forest of companionship along the river.

A night in the ER, a lesson in Buddhism, makes a man grateful for life itself, the basic stuff, coffee, an apple, the English language, and the memory of cousin Dorothy telling me about my grandpa, a book in his left hand, the reins in his right, as he rode the mower out to cut hay. He loved poetry and so did she because she loved him.

So did Rozel. He once saw a poem I wrote and said, "Your grandpa would be proud of you." A blessing passed down from the beyond.

All of my elders are gone who taught me from the Bible and I am on my own. I pray they found their heavenly home. I believe in a fraction of what I was taught, my faith wavers. My faithful older brother whom I could talk to about these things went skating one day, slipped, hit his head, and died, and now I am much older than he, which is not right. I do know that when Jesus, surrounded by the sick and impoverished and blind and demon-possessed, said to His disciples, "Whatsoever you do for the least of these, you do for me and your Father in heaven," He spoke the truth, and if you wish for some plain simple truth in your life, along with your interesting attitudes and opinions, this is the one to accept, and you'll find it on the street and in the ER.

I was in the ER for almost 24 hours and did not bother the nurses to ask to use the toilet and as I left I stopped at the men's room and took pleasure in a good strong piss, and I feel that pleasure every day since, not for me the pitiful old-man's dribble but the real thing, me standing at my stanchion like a Percheron, pissing into the center of the pool to give off the sound of a waterfall, and 15 feet away, on the other side of the closed door, my woman hears it and after I zip up and flush and exit, she looks at me with appreciation, grateful to have me here, ready to defend the house against Mongol horsemen or escaped desperadoes or Second Amendment lunatics, I the Urinator will piss them away. Or so I believe, though I haven't mentioned it to her.

The antidote for self-pity is to witness real suffering and maybe this is a motive for going to work for the PD and FD and becoming an EMT or RN or MD, to recognize suffering up close and come home to peace and order and cheerful goodwill. I was only a tourist. And it could've been otherwise, which someday it will be but not yet. Home felt exhilarating, like Emily in *Our Town*—"Oh, earth, you're too wonderful for anybody to realize you." As she says, "Do any human beings ever realize life while they live it—every, every minute?" No, not every minute, a person has to go through airport security, shower and shave, get your teeth cleaned, read the obituaries, take care of other matters, but I realize life more resplendently after my night in the ER. That Sunday I wrote in the margin of the church bulletin:

The words appear with a whistle
Like the sound of an incoming missile.
It's so good to hear it,
"Let us live in the Spirit,"
From Romans, St. Paul's epistle.

Death's Door, 1813, after William Blake

Lying in the ER I thought that when my end comes I should make it a good and memorable death and not lie in bed complaining but sit up on my deathbed and be a font of wise sayings, one aphorism after another. All good things come to an end. Nothing is ever accidental. Nothing so bad in which there is not some good. No summer without winter. Time waits for no man. Me today and you tomorrow. God never shuts one door but what He opens another.

Not every question has an answer. Everyone is the judge of their own good luck. Small sorrows speak and great sorrow is silent. Death pays all debts. In the end, it's our job to disappear.

My daughter will ask, "Can I get you anything?" and I'll say, "If wishes were horses and beggars could ride, the world would be drowned in a sea of pride." When someone asks how I feel, I'll say, "Death is bad enough but thank God I don't need to attend the memorial service."

My decline, decrepitude, and death are not a tragedy, not even a small one. The impoverished children playing in a park and finding used hypodermics and thereby contracting HIV: that is a tragedy. You read it in the paper and the heart breaks. The desperate Mexican and Guatemalan migrants who paid a smuggler thousands of dollars and he drove 25 of them jammed in a Ford SUV over the border and onto the California desert where he ran a stop sign and crashed into a Peterbilt truck and 13 bodies lay scattered on the highway, dead, Yesenia Melendrez Cardona, dead in the arms of her mother crying out in Spanish, brushing the blood from her daughter's beautiful face, Yesenia, 23, the same age as my daughter, this is tragedy. Let's be clear about these things.

I was born in this country to a mail clerk and a housewife, two soft-spoken Christians, a mother who loved comedians, and Mr. Buehler pulled me off the power saw and sent me to Speech and after college, having no particular job skills, I got a job in radio by virtue of being willing to get up in the dark on winter mornings and be cheerful on the air. I visited Nashville to see the Grand Ole Opry and came home and suggested starting a live music show on Saturday nights and the boss Bill Kling said, "Go ahead." My story in 100 words. And now, on a sunny Saturday morning, I walk out in Central Park and sense widespread amiability afoot, people walking their dogs and small children happy to be out of a tiny apartment, old folks at rest on benches, joggers, strollers, amblers, and I think I could pull 20 of them together and rehearse them in "New York, New York, it's a heck of a town, the Bronx is up and the Battery's down, the people ride in a hole in the ground." I'd say, "I'm making a video for my class in cognitive empathy in urban communities," and thus, knowing it's not a joke, they'd link arms in a dance line and do it and really get into it and feel the companionship and love of comrades that Whitman wrote about, except by a reservoir, not a river.

The Tornado, 1811, Pavel Petrovich Svinin

4
~

LEGACY IS POSTERITY'S VIEW OF YOUR POSTERIOR AND ONE POSTERIOR LOOKS MUCH LIKE ANOTHER

The Writing Master, 1882, Thomas Eakins

Face it. Life is brief, sometimes momentary. History is not about you and me. We die and we disappear. We lie in the care center and our caregiver removes the cellphone from our clutches and we thereby cease to be an American individual and become a creature not so different from a muskrat or possum. There is no such thing as Legacy unless you're Stalin or Chaplin or Chopin or my cousin Katharine Hepburn, people on that level, otherwise you are a name on a stone soon to be moldy and forgotten like the other lambs who went astray. Billionaires put their names on enormous stone façades of temples of art and learning but nobody notices the names as they enter, everyone is looking down at the steps. People who look up to admire the famous name are likely to fall and require medical attention. There is a lesson here.

I had some big times and remember them pretty clearly. The Saturday at Tanglewood when 14,000 came through the gates and Leo Kottke played and the pianist Hsing-ay Hsu did some showstoppers of Liszt, Dvořák, and Debussy and Fred Newman gargled "The Flight of the Bumblebee" and afterward the crowd hung around and we sang "Bye Bye, Love" and then a soulful "Amazing Grace," which really was amazing and a woman fell off the chair she was standing on, hit her head, was knocked unconscious, and I said, "Is there a doctor in the house?" and there was a whole line of them, meanwhile we sang about the 10,000 Years, the Fear verse, and "Through many dangers, toils, and cares we have already come." The woman stood up and waved and we cheered and sang about the chariot swinging low and, for some reason, "In My Life." We went to a cabin in the woods for a party with the crew, which lasted until 1:30 a.m., after a day that began at 7 a.m., and the next morning on the veranda of the Red Lion Inn in Lenox, I drank my coffee and reflected on the show and had the same regrets I had after every show I ever did. It's Not Good Enough. It never was. It was the Brethren in me. No critic was half so severe as I on myself. A big pleasure on Saturday turned sour on Sunday and thus perpetual dissatisfaction drives the bus forward.

And now I have no regret. At 79, I'm done with it. My good conservative Crandall ancestors were driven out of New England because 1774 was the wrong time to speak up for law and order. And their neighbors, seeing which way the wind was blowing, drove them away and stole their homes and livestock. Up in New Brunswick, the Crandalls married the impoverished Keillors, an illiterate lot newly arrived from Yorkshire, and had the story been otherwise and my conservative ancestors forsaken principle and joined the revolution, where would I be? I'd be a Connecticut multibillionaire living in a 40-room mansion with a major OxyContin habit, drifting half-conscious in decadent grandeur, being fleeced by a bevy of sycophants. And I would've been cheated of my Keillorhood, which gives me persistence. I'm glad to be where I am, thank you.

The Little Fortune, 1495, Albrecht Dürer

No regrets and I don't think about death at all. Why pitch a fit about the inevitable? I'm old. What else is new? A plane crash would be horrible, all that screaming, but I'll likely go down well-medicated in a quiet room, but it's not up to me. I was brought up by stoics. At our high school in Anoka, the teams were nicknamed the Tornadoes after the town was hit by two devastating tornadoes back in the Thirties, a brilliant idea, to adopt a terrifying disaster as a sign of strength. People died in those storms and you could argue that the nickname is disrespectful to the dead, but it strikes me as bold, rather than taking the name of imaginary threats such as Lions and Bears or

Gophers. So just call me Coronary Keillor and get out of my way. I am no pushover.

When I was young I thought of death a lot, thanks to my evangelical upbringing. Gospel preachers' big selling point was the prospect of imminent death, the Titanic was mentioned frequently, cars struck by speeding trains, flash floods, devastating fires. God's love for humanity was only a footnote, the preacher aimed to make you feel that the church could explode at any moment, the basement was filling with leaking gas, a little spark would blow us sky-high, or maybe a meteorite the size of Vermont was hurtling through space with our address on it, that was the gist of the sermon. And then in college I wrote all those dark stories in which good people died suddenly and ironically, and now, though I've passed the average life expectancy of a published memoirist, I don't think about my own demise. It's of no particular interest.

Not that I feel immortal, I don't. I'm a daddy mouse in a cornfield, shopping for my family, and suddenly there will be a rush of wings and a huge shadow and I'll feel the claws in my back as I rise high in the air. But a person doesn't need to keep looking up at the sky, you can be cool about death, like the engineer at the guillotine who said, "Hand me the pliers, I see the problem." I have that joke and two good Ole & Lena jokes about death that I hope to be able to tell the ambulance crew.

My Maker has His eye on me along with the sparrow, deciding which of us to summon when, and meanwhile these are very good years and if you're lucky and make it this far, prepare to be delighted. I stood at a urinal and felt the flow and stepped back and the automatic flush went *whooshhhh* and it was a joyful sound like when you walk onto a plaza and a flock of pigeons rises up in a cloud of wings pounding and you can't help but feel uplifted. I often feel this way but with more appreciation for delight than when I was young and thinking about exigencies. I look at men's fashion ads and here sit handsome twentyish guys in expensive clothes looking anguished, as if their novel had just been rejected by Knopf. Compared to that, I feel great, never better.

Of course some mornings the brain is slow, the gut remorseful, the heart flutters, but that is only for dramatic interest. Every life needs rough water, otherwise where's the story? But when I feel lousy, I do as my wife does, I go out for a walk. A person doesn't learn much driving around in a car, but you go for a walk and feel the surge and flow of life, the ladies power walking and ancients shuffling along, reluctant to give up, and the dog walkers and the toddlers thrilled to be afoot, smokers here and there banished to the street, and women of transcendent beauty whom a man must remind himself not to look at for more than five seconds. I walk briskly to 72nd Street and descend to the subway platform, which is packed, which pleases me—some of the job of waiting has been done by others—and in a minute, a train comes clattering in, the local. Should I take it or wait for the express? I board the local. I'm a Minnesotan, I commuted by car for years, so the train is excitement, I feel like a 10-year-old. I like to stand in the front window of the first car, looking ahead down the tracks at the oncoming beams and switches. I keep expecting the express to pass, one more wrong choice in my life, but it doesn't.

I look over my fellow passengers, particularly the elegant dancer in black tights and the goofus with bad hair and a big schnozz. They talk, she touches his forearm, there is some relationship, but what? He is wiping his nose with the back of his hand and it bothers her. She hands him a tissue. She stands up to get off at 50th and whispers to him and presses some money into his hand. I think she's his older sister.

I get off at 42nd Street and walk through the station and hear a string quartet playing Mozart's *Eine Kleine Nachtmusik* with great energy, and I stop to drop a bill in the open violin case, a bill that, as it falls, I see is a $20 bill, more than I'd intended to give, but what cheapskate would reach down into the kitty for change, Mozart in the subway is a miracle. The four, two women, two men, are in their twenties, one of them looks up and smiles. I stop to get my money's worth. I'm an old man. Crowds pass in a rush, all of them young and in a hurry, and I, partly because I need to catch my breath, get to appreciate this quartet, which is, I swear, *really good* and they're playing for free and as you hustle through the station, you can smell hot dogs and hear pure genius over the rumble of machinery—the wonder of Manhattan, Whitman could've written about this, and in his memory I drop another $20 in the case. Back when I was young, I was too important to notice this and now I'm not and I do. Simple as that.

I hear snatches of Japanese and a little bit of Swedish passing, and some parents steering their teenagers along, dazed parents who I think maybe are from the Midwest, accustomed to being wrapped in a steel automobile so they're wary of being on foot among strangers, and they don't seem to realize the Mozart is being played by living people in real time. I clamber up the stairs to Times Square, Neon National Park, and it's exhilarating for an old writer to be out in a crowd of people. The world is larger and more varied than I ever imagined, beyond my comprehension. A Black evangelist in a blue polyester suit paces the corner of 42nd & Fifth Avenue, a massive Bible in one hand, and he bellows at the river of humanity, which shrinks away from him. "Do you know where you will spend Eternity? Do you know? Let me tell you!" he cries.

I'd like to stop and chat with him—he is of a vanishing tribe of the Lord's foot soldiers, perhaps the last living street evangelist in Manhattan—but he has his work to do and I have mine. Mine is to go up the stairs past the stone lions and up to the magnificent Rose Reading Room and sit at a long table with green study lamps among people in their twenties, many of them Asian, perhaps children of immigrants, studying textbooks, perhaps to become lawyers or doctors or engineers and fulfill the dream of their mothers who work in nail salons. This is a sacred place where the loving sacrifices of the saints are redeemed by the children. The walls are lined with shelves of thick tomes and nobody pulls a book out to peruse, they are only here to create a holy silence. I am here to write about the grandeur of my daily life, which now I am doing. My words don't suffice, but I am persistent. I head down the winding marble staircase, hanging on to the brass rail. I am so very careful. My mother told me to be and now at 79 I am obedient. I had to live to be old before I could appreciate what a paradise this is. Inscribe this in your heart, reader: whenever you feel sad, get out and take a hike.

God had a plan that I had to have a career first and get that out of the way so that I could retire and fully enjoy this day, an ordinary Thursday, but no day is ordinary ever again. Yes, chronology is God's plan. God did not allow the internet to be invented in the 16th century because then there would've been no Renaissance, no Reformation, we'd be watching YouTube in a crude earthen hut surrounded by our animals, sending emails in Middle English, and Mozart would've been playing video games and never written *Don Giovanni*. All my life I've been waiting to be old enough to take hold of life and now I'm here and it's beautiful.

Someone will write a history of the late 20th century that shows everything I believed true was a bushel of sheep manure soaked in horse piss and sprinkled with rabbit turds. Wrong, wrong, wrong. Up was down and right was left and my tribe was the losing side. Okay, whatever, no problem. It's a pleasure to take off your badge and uniform and just observe the world go by. Let the young take over and I will unload the dishwasher and reorganize my sock drawer. Now and then my wife hands me an odd dish, a platter or colander, a hypotenuse, and says, "Can you put this on that top shelf?" and I do. It's an easy reach for me and it feels good to have a purpose.

One day I walked up Amsterdam past 91st and heard a woman say, "Mr. Wobegon" and it was an old lady standing in front of Central Baptist, waiting to go in for the Friday night service, so I stopped and said hello. Her name was Angie and she remembered having seen me once on TV a long time ago telling a story about how I was fascinated by a flock of geese flying just above and ahead of my car as I drove down the highway, so fascinated that when they angled off to the right, I drove into the ditch. One little detail in a story many years before stuck with her. This moved me more than if I'd gotten a Pulitzer Prize. Prizes are purely political, each one more political than the next, but this little encounter was from the heart. A real woman saw me and remembered a story I told and I was awestruck. Back when I was cool I avoided awe but at 79 I'm struck by it often. Cast your bread upon the waters. She didn't know my name but she remembered the flock of birds, my hood ornament, and me following them into the ditch. (A true story, it was a shallow ditch, I drove down into it and then up out of it.) Her face lit up, it made her very happy to make this connection while waiting for prayer meeting to start. I walked on, feeling that my life was now worthwhile. Less is more, and amusing her was a good enough justification for being.

One Sunday morning, on my way to church, I got caught up

in a crowd flowing into a Catholic church and I went with the flow into a Spanish Mass, crowded into a pew, kneeling next to a weeping woman with a bright blue and silver scarf over her head. I come from fundamentalists and we were all doctrine, no mystery, and we held the world at arm's length and here I was in a mystery, worshipping with the handymen and cleaning ladies, and for all that I couldn't understand, I felt in my heart. God help us. Give these good people some comfort and happiness in this country. The woman weeping next to me leaned my way, and I prayed for her prayers to be answered. Thank you for it all, Lord, good, bad, indivisible, invisible. And thank you for leading me in here.

Back in my folkie days, we sang a Carter Family song, "This world is not my home, I'm just a-passing through," though we knew little about homelessness, and now at almost 80 I know a little more. Electronic wonders are a mystery to me and when I open an instruction manual, it's a highway to hell and in five minutes I am moaning like a wounded raccoon. The front page of the paper is half-unrecognizable, sometimes two-thirds, dangerous treacherous people in high places who cannot possibly be serious, lunatic carelessness in politics, our society's contempt for the natural world reaching a boiling point, scientists using the word "uninhabitable," meanwhile the wicked are beautifully disciplined and dedicated while the righteous are confused and at odds with each other.

For half my lifetime, the idiocy of supply-side economics—that prosperity is created from the top down, by cutting taxes on the rich and running obscene deficits and tolerating third-world poverty for more and more of our people—has corrupted government, perhaps beyond the possibility of reform. It turned two Democratic presidents, Clinton and Obama, into moderate Republicans, and maybe Biden will fall to it too, but the young will need to solve this, not us. We have the wrong experience for the job, like sending a crew of proctologists to explore the moons of Uranus. We are tourists. We shouldn't be allowed to vote. We need to go away. Gays and lesbians enjoy the freedom to marry today because a couple million Americans who would rather die than see same-sex marriages went ahead and died. Our turn is coming soon. Maybe I'd serve society better by eating more triple cheeseburgers and hot fudge sundaes. If necessary, I could manage that.

I do believe reform will come through the efforts of people who know the goodness of life, not from rage and resentment, but my opinion doesn't matter so forget that I said it.

The world that's coming may not please us but that's okay, we'll be heading out the door to the graveyard. Maybe the Scandinavians of Minnesota will need to demasculinize their surnames (Olson, Peterson, Hansen, Rasmussen) and become matrimonial. Pronoun laws will require him, her, us, it, everyone, nobody, somebody, several, many, few, to indicate clearly our orientation or occidentalism. Maybe Los Angeles will become LaCosta to be nonthreatening to agnostics, and St. Paul become East Minneapolis. The navigator Amerigo Vespucci, for whom America is named, was hardly respectful toward indigenous peoples so the country will become simply US. Columbia needs to be stricken and Washington. He was a general who got lucky and trapped the British at Yorktown and won the war, meanwhile he kept slaves. Rename the city Emerson for the man who said, "This time, like all times, is a very good one if we but know what to do with it." Statues must fall, and why should our largest city go on memorializing the Duke of York? Huckleberry Finn is out, gone, kaput, *ausgeschlossen*, so is Chaucer, and your opinion and mine are not needed so shut your mouth and go bake your cornbread and pluck your banjo and shoo the chickens out of the magnolias. And let us contemplate this: we were terribly lucky to have lived when we did. I tell myself this several times a day. There was genocide, stupidity on a mass scale, insane wars, but growing up in Minnesota with a book in one hand, a baseball glove in the other, a boy could be so innocent and unself-conscious. It was beautiful. I miss it. But you didn't hear it because I didn't say what I just said.

The enumeration of blessings is a daily ritual of my old age. Mine always begins with my parents, John and Grace, and includes the click in my heart valve that made Dr. Mork excuse me from football the year before Mr. Buehler kicked me out of shop class and into Miss Person's speech class. It includes various romances and especially the lunch at Docks in 1992 with my sister's classmate's sister—a freelance violinist enduring semi-poverty out of her love of classical music—that turned into marriage. I crave leadership and she provides it, keeping me out of restaurants where the only vegetables are pickles, French fries, and onions. I quit drinking 20 years ago in order to spare her from having to beg me to. I read my stuff to her and if she doesn't respond, I dump it. She tells me if there's spinach in my teeth. "Smile," she says, and I try to. She is a quasi-vegan and so I am too except when she's in New York and I'm in Minnesota when I hunker down with other hairy illiterates by a blazing fire and hack at the half-raw hunk of antelope and speak in short sentences separated by grunts and belches. In the book of Acts, God lowers a great blanket from heaven on which are many animals, sheep, pigs, cows, and God tells Peter, "Kill and eat." It couldn't be any clearer than that. I considered veganism once when I passed a truckload of hogs on the highway and imagined their suffering, but the solution is simple: luxury coaches with AC and pig bunks.

My 79th year has led me into the fields of serenity, which is the peace Jesus promised to His people in place of the world's tribulation. I mention serenity here at the end of the book because serenity is the most boring subject on earth aside from math. It's a quiet summer day in which a cup of ginger tea is a highlight and then my wife's beautiful shoulders where she stands in the kitchen slicing onions for the salad and I feel like singing "Celeste Aida" and don't because she's holding a knife and what if she forgets which opera this is from so I go back to the ballgame and here, with runners on first and second, Max Kepler lays down a perfect bunt 20 feet down the third baseline and the pitcher has to dash over and throw a perfect fastball to first to catch him by a split second and meanwhile the runners have advanced. To a man in a serene state of mind, a perfect bunt is more beautiful than a home run. Finesse beats power. It's good to feel this good.

One night I had a dream in which the beauty of old age was made clear to me. A crowd of old friends on a Minnesota farm, people playing music in the yard, a picnic, a softball game, and I recognized old hippie pals from the Seventies who had dropped out of the rat race to pursue independence and endure poverty to be able to play hammered dulcimer, make quilts, write poetry, throw pots, paint, carve, sculpt, pay attention to the natural world, some of them acting out of Christian conviction, some ambitious to achieve, some in search of elusive truth, all of them in flight from regimentation and officious jargon, but in the dream it wasn't the Seventies, we were in our seventies, and it hit me—it still does, even harder—that at 79 I've finally arrived and am living the life I wanted when I was 25 and dropped out of grad school, walked away from a dull easy job to become a writer, and here we all were a half-century later, free as the wind, free of pretense, loving our delicious lives, every hour, my communard friends Gregory and Terese Melis and Howard and Jody Mohr and Louis and Ann Jenkins and Carol Bly, and my wife the violinist was there, the most independent person I know.

Finally living the life we looked for in our romantic twenties is a vision of old age unlike any other. Thanks to Social Security, Medicare, pension, some savings, the perks of seniority, we're finally free to stroll through the fields of delight, paying attention. We got distracted before by kids, careers, good causes, status consciousness, lawn care, our commitment to support the arts, and now we only have a precious life to live. God has blessed us.

I believe this with my whole heart. I've made up many stories in my so-called career but now I'm talking truth. When I'm finished writing this book—*I'm almost there, I promise*—I'll walk out the door and across the street and into the park and I will be prepared to be blessed.

I didn't choose serenity, it chose me in 2019 when COVID came along with the fear of contagion. The more I read about the virus, the less I cared to experience it personally and lie in a hospital with a hose in my throat. Old people were dying by the scores in nursing homes so I stayed home with my vigilant wife, otherwise I might be hanging out in saloons singing sea chanteys and freely sharing bacteria. Instead, she and I led a cloistered life, reading books, eating salads, playing Scrabble. I'd been scheduled to host a Caribbean cruise and it got canceled and so did everything else. I woke up in the morning with a free day ahead and free days as far into the future as I could see. I came to enjoy the quarantine life. It is a good test of marriage and perhaps should be made a requirement for getting a license, thirty (30) days secluded in a small apartment to see how the couple feels about each other afterward. Seclusion with my wife made me appreciate her beautiful heart and good humor even more. Falling in love is an exquisite state of stupidity and to have made such a wise choice in one's stupor is excellent good luck.

Church was closed in the pandemic but I went to Morning Prayer on Zoom and one morning we read the verse in Romans in which Paul says that the Holy Spirit prays for us "in accordance with the will of God," and this dazzling thought that God Himself is praying for us burst over me like a Roman candle. I'd been brought up with the idea of an angry God stoking the fires of hell and writing our sins in the Big Book and here was another idea entirely. An omniscient and omnipotent God who is praying to Himself for our redemption this is the Benevolence of Creation in a nutshell. So I thought. It was 7 a.m. and I was on my first cup of coffee and I felt truly blessed.

The Apostle Paul, ca. 1657, Rembrandt van Rijn

I'd been a busy man for many years and acquired a restless mind and when that life collapsed, I gained a silence that would've been a problem for me in my hustling twenties but in my seventies is a blessing, pure and simple. When you've been running hard on a treadmill for years, serenity comes as a complete surprise, same as if you pitch a tent and sleep on the ground and eat burnt food in a rainstorm and are awakened by bears grunting as they rip open your backpacks, after which you're prepared to appreciate a hotel room with a bed and toilet and shower with hot water.

I look at the newspaper and there is no serenity to be found there. In our democracy, powerful forces are at work in behalf of privileged minorities and against the interests of the upcoming generations. It has always been so, privilege had to be toppled and torn down, privilege seldom stepped aside willingly. I accept my WASPish responsibility for my sins and my ancestors' and predecessors who cheated the Dakotah of the land my apartment building sits on in Minneapolis.

The Dakotah were nomadic hunters and we Anglos were carpenters and gardeners who wanted to put up fences, so when we outnumbered the nomads we rewrote the rules in our favor. It's an interesting story. My building has now put up a fence to keep homeless people from camping on our lawn. For all I know, some of them may be Dakotah descendants. I was out for a walk the other day and saw a man sleeping on a bench at a bus stop, a suitcase beside him. This is not our WASP way of life. You can do it up north, pitch a tent in the woods, but not in a neighborhood of apartment buildings. Living within four walls and ceiling with a door that locks is basic to our culture. Climate is a factor and also the locked door gives us freedom from having to worry about intruders and to think about the goodness of life instead, work, family, comedy, liberty, poetry, the laws of physics, the basic elements that go to make up the ideal cheeseburger. I don't apologize for our culture, I only wish we'd been not so nasty.

I come from the era when we had a sense of cultural membership and knew the same songs and a year ago I stood in front of a crowd and we sang about the amber waves of grain, about working on the railroad and Dinah in the kitchen, the grasshopper picking his teeth with a carpet tack, and looking over Jordan and seeing a band of angels, and the elderly sang along happily and the young looked for the lyrics on their smartphones. When you need Google to tell you this is the land of the pilgrims' pride where your fathers died, I wonder what the world is coming to, but it's not my business, I'm a tourist here.

Serenity tells me to let it be, walk softly, improve the day, lighten up, leave anguish to the editorial columnists. Old age is the cure for self-importance. You listen to voices in the wind and they are calm and humorous, none of them urge you to put on a helmet and pick up a sword. I lived through the Era of Agitation, when we were militant against all sins except our own and it was followed by the Era of

Running and Purification, each to their own gait, feeling a common bond of perspiration and odor and now I'm in the Era of Gathering Thoughts. I am a philosopher sitting under my tree and I find reasons to love this world and my heart is lifted.

Peaceable Kingdom, ca. 1830–32, Edward Hicks

I am a lucky man, luck has followed me like a friendly dog and though I can be as sorrowful as the next person, humor is where I hang my hat. Growing up Sanctified Brethren gave me a solemn face so people often ask, "Are you okay?" as if I might be in pain, which I am not. I feel buoyant in the morning and sit down to the task at hand, which is what I'm doing right now. This. What you're reading. I walked away from two marriages and escaped the heaviness of the failure to make another person happy and I got out of town, in search of light-heartedness, which I believe in. Power and influence are temporary, charisma is an illusion, brilliance depends on who's writing the test, but buoyancy is a gift of God's grace. The race is not necessarily to the swift nor the battle to the strong nor health to people who follow the rules but it is in our power to rise above circumstance and improve the day, and luck is a necessity born of persistence.

It's what happened to Bud Mueller in Lake Wobegon who was on his way to the Sidetrack Tap to drown his sorrows when a hundred-pound stone plaque fell off the façade of the Central Building and would've killed him outright but he had just stopped and turned because Mrs. Burkert mistook him for her daughter Donna's boyfriend Merle, a friend of Bud's. Mistaken identity saved his life. So when Merle drank a six-pack of St. Wendell's beer and a pint of Jim Beam on a dare one night and ran his car off the road and was killed, Bud married Donna and does his best to make her happy and sometimes succeeds and intends to keep trying.

Peace and Plenty, 1865, George Inness

This has happened to me all my life since as a boy I was very quiet, which led people to imagine that I was brilliant and I worked this mistaken impression very hard and Mr. Buehler stepped in and saved me from self-destruction and Miss Person laughed at my speeches and nobody laid a hand on me in anger and I was a good listener and heard the cheerful chirps and murmurs that lie at the heart of language, the sweet drizzle of small talk, and when I lucked my way into radio, I made it into an art form, the solo conversation known as The News from Lake Wobegon. Now I'm a wary old man, stepping into the morning shower, aware of old men who slipped on wet tile and banged their heads and jarred the cranial material so they now don't know the Lord's Prayer or the teams of the American League or the directions to and from Kowalski's, but I shower safely and dry off and put on my jeans and black T-shirt, and go to work, which now that I have finished writing this book, which was fun, I must get back to the screenplay I've been thinking about, a comedy in which there are five funerals at which a man is asked to give eulogies for old enemies. Thanks for your company. Be well. Keep in touch. Do good work.

Every day is a beautiful gift,
Tender and precious and swift.
The light and the sound,
The sky and the ground,
Every hour cries out to be lived.
Though I may be over the hill,
Still I think I can and I will.
I've forgotten just what
I can and will, but
They remain a goal of mine still.

Every year I pass the date
When my balloon shall deflate.
My mom entered heaven
At age ninety-seven,
And I aim to reach ninety-eight.
But if the shadows should fall
Tomorrow and I get the call,
I hope to have time
To speak one last line:
Thank you, Lord. Thanks for it all.

CREDITS

p. 9 Courtesy National Gallery of Art, Washington.

p. 20 Courtesy National Gallery of Art, Washington.

p. 23 Courtesy National Gallery of Art, Washington.

p. 25 Courtesy National Gallery of Art, Washington.

p. 31 The Metropolitan Museum of Art, New York.

p. 35 Courtesy National Gallery of Art, Washington.

p. 42 The Metropolitan Museum of Art, New York.

p. 47 The Metropolitan Museum of Art, New York.

p. 48 The Metropolitan Museum of Art, New York.

p. 61 Courtesy National Gallery of Art, Washington.

p. 71 From *The Mechanism of Human Facial Expression* by
     Guillaume-Benjamin-Amand Duchenne de Boulogne.
     Courtesy National Gallery of Art, Washington.

p. 76 From "The Grave," a poem by Robert Blair, 1813, after William Blake.
     The Metropolitan Museum of Art, New York.

p. 78 The Metropolitan Museum of Art, New York.

p. 79 The Metropolitan Museum of Art, New York.

p. 81 The Metropolitan Museum of Art, New York.

p. 92 Courtesy National Gallery of Art, Washington.

p. 94 The Metropolitan Museum of Art, New York.

p. 95 The Metropolitan Museum of Art, New York.